Christmas at the Ranch

Other books By Stacey Lee Powell

Strings of Hope

Get Off The Dating Apps! Journal to Find Your Soul Mate

Christmas at the Ranch

Novel Written by
Stacey Lee Powell

Edited by
Krissy Smith

Based on the movie written by
Julie Anton and Christin Baker

Directed by
Christin Baker

Tello Books

Christmas at the Ranch

Copyright © 2024 Stacey Lee Powell

All rights reserved.

No part of this book may be reproduced, stored in a retrieval system, or transmitted in any form or by any means without the prior written permission of the publisher, except as permitted by law.

This book is a work of fiction. Names, characters, places, and events are products of the author's imagination or are used fictitiously. Any resemblance to actual events, locales, or persons, living or dead, is purely coincidental.

Based on the movie *Christmas at the Ranch*, written by Julie Anton and directed by Christin Baker.

Second Edition

Published by Tello Books

Christmas at the Ranch

Novel Written by
Stacey Lee Powell

Edited by
Krissy Smith

Based on the movie written by
Julie Anton and Christin Baker

Directed by
Christin Baker

Tello Books

Christmas at the Ranch

Copyright © 2024 Stacey Lee Powell

All rights reserved.

No part of this book may be reproduced, stored in a retrieval system, or transmitted in any form or by any means without the prior written permission of the publisher, except as permitted by law.

This book is a work of fiction. Names, characters, places, and events are products of the author's imagination or are used fictitiously. Any resemblance to actual events, locales, or persons, living or dead, is purely coincidental.

Based on the movie *Christmas at the Ranch*, written by Julie Anton and directed by Christin Baker.

Second Edition

Published by Tello Books

Chapter 1

As dawn kissed the sprawling Hollis Hills Ranch, Kate, a seasoned ranch hand in her late twenties stood near the vibrant red barn, taking in the crisp morning air. The 100 acres of rolling pastures and shaded woodlands glowed in the soft light, a sanctuary of peace and stillness. Yet even here, surrounded by open land and the gentle hum of life, questions lingered in her mind, breaking through the quiet.

The ranch's main house stood just beyond, its wraparound porch glowing warmly in the sunrise. Rocking chairs invited rest, but Kate couldn't stop. There was work to do, routines to follow, and a restlessness she couldn't shake. The ranch might be her refuge, but it couldn't keep the outside world at bay forever.

She was already deep into her morning routine and took a deep breath, letting the crisp morning air fill her lungs. Out here in the stillness of the ranch, she felt a kind of peace she could never quite explain to anyone else. The quiet, the animals, the open land—it let her just be. But even with that peace, there were questions she couldn't shake.

The rhythm of the morning chores helped keep her mind busy, but it was still easy to get lost in thought. After three years, she could make her way to the chicken coop with her eyes closed. It sat nestled on the land, a cozy home for the hens who laid their eggs faithfully each night. Kate lifted the door and smiled as she gathered the fresh eggs. Everything here had its purpose, its rhythm. Yet, no matter how comforting that was, a nagging thought always lingered in the back of her mind: Is this it?

Kate shifted her focus to her favorite part of the morning: caring for Louie, her horse. She brushed his coat with gentle strokes, whispering soft words as she led him from the barn to the exercise pen. The feel of Louie's coat beneath her hands brought a sense of calm. At least with you I know what love feels like, she thought, a bittersweet feeling tugging at her. She didn't have anyone waiting for her at the end of the day—just the ranch, just Louie. Maybe that was enough. But, deep down, she wasn't so sure anymore.

As Kate rode Louie across the ranch, her mind kept spinning. This morning was worse than most—the feeling that she was meant for something more gnawed at her. Her silhouette cut through the golden light of the early morning as they passed a towering oak tree standing tall in the middle of the fields. The sight of it always calmed her. There was strength in being rooted, in staying grounded, just like that tree. But was she truly rooted, or just stuck? She used to think she knew the answer, but now... she wasn't so sure.

Lost in thought, Kate found herself perched atop a hill, overlooking the sprawling expanse below. With practiced ease, she dismounted Louie and reached for her thermos of coffee and an apple from her saddlebag. This is it, she thought, taking a slow sip of the steaming coffee as her eyes swept over the land. This is the life people dream of. And yet, the familiar ache lingered inside her, that gnawing feeling that something was missing.

***

Across the country in San Francisco, Haley, also in her late twenties, lay sprawled in bed in her sleek but cramped apartment. Her face pressed into a silk pillowcase, hovering in that space between sleep and wakefulness. Another morning, another fire to put out, she thought as her phone buzzed endlessly on the nightstand. She hated how tied she was to that little glowing screen—how her whole life seemed to revolve around it. When did this become my life? She wondered. Haley knew she was good at her job, but lately, success felt... empty.

Her phone kept lighting up with notifications—social media, texts, and missed calls from Charlie, her brother. It all painted a picture of a life so full yet, somehow, draining. Haley rubbed her eyes and groaned, swiping through the chaos on her screen.

She should be grateful—her career was thriving after all. But lately, it all felt so hollow. The stress, the pressure, the constant demands... Do I even want this anymore? The thought lingered, unsettling. What else could there be? This life was all she knew these days.

It had been almost ten years since she'd left the ranch behind for college, trading open fields and horses for skyscrapers and boardrooms. The city had become her world, not Hollis Hills Ranch. She'd been back only for Paw Paw's funeral and some holidays, brief visits that never quite felt like home. But as the years passed, she couldn't shake the feeling that something was missing.

For a moment, she considered tossing her phone back on the nightstand and crawling back under the covers. But she was already behind. Not just with work, but in life. Every part of her existence felt like a fire she had to keep putting out. Why can't I just unplug for one day? Is that really too much to ask? The thought alone made her anxious, like the whole world might crumble if she stepped away, even if for just a moment.

She took a deep breath and climbed out of bed. One more meeting, one more deadline, and maybe then I'll finally breathe. But she knew better. There would always be something else. The word "stop" hadn't been part of her vocabulary for a long time.

Thirty minutes later, she was dressed and weaving through the busy sidewalk, her gaze locked on the screen as she fired off frantic replies. Mega NRG, a fast-growing beverage startup, was just steps away. Known for its bold branding, louder-than-life flavors, and a relentless hustle culture aimed squarely at the "bro" demographic, it was a world that thrived on adrenaline and disruption. Haley had left a stable, well-paying corporate job to take a chance here, betting on the opportunity to get in on the ground floor of something game-changing.

It wasn't even 9 a.m., and she was already dealing with firing Carl. He kept pleading for another chance, but all she could think about, as his voice filtered through her ears, was how nothing felt right anymore. When had she last felt truly happy?

Inside the bustling offices of Mega NRG Drink, late morning brought a flurry of activity. Haley strode in, her focus already divided between her phone call, Carl wasn't giving up easily, and the busy morning routine unfolding around her. Across the room, Steve, her assistant, sat at his desk seemingly engrossed in his work as Haley approached.

"Yes, Carl, I get the joke," Haley spoke into her phone, her tone a mixture of frustration and exasperation. "But you've already accidentally tweeted a few times from the company's account. So far, our followers have seen your Tinder pictures, an admittedly very cute video of your cat, and now a lazy joke about getting crabs from a diner."

A hint of amusement danced in Steve's eyes as he glanced up from his desk and waved. Haley waved back, phone pressed to her ear, her voice firm but tinged with regret. "This is a start-up, Carl, and our social media presence matters."

She paused, her eyes scanning the office hallway as Carl's muffled protests crackled through the line. Her lips tightened, and she took a measured breath before continuing. "Yes, of course, we're letting you go. I'm sorry."

Haley passed by Steve's desk, her pace slowing for a moment. Her free hand gripped the edge of her tote bag, fingers drumming nervously against the leather. Carl's voice rose, defensive and desperate, but she cut in before he could spiral further.

"This will give you more time to focus on your stand-up," she added, her tone sharp but still polite.

Reaching her office door, she stopped and leaned against the frame for a beat, closing her eyes briefly as Carl's pleas turned into an awkward pitch. She rolled her eyes skyward, muttering under her breath before speaking again. "No, Carl, I will not come to your improv show."

She pushed the door open, stepping inside with the phone still to her ear. The weariness in her voice deepened as she softened her tone just slightly. "You'll be hearing from HR. I do wish you the best, though."

With a decisive click, she ended the call and dropped her phone onto the desk, her expression reflecting a mixture of relief and exhaustion. She exhaled, eyes closing for a brief second as if to gather herself before finally sitting down at her desk.

A few minutes later, the sound of a soft knock broke her brief reprieve. Steve, grinning as usual, stood in her doorway holding a coffee in one hand and a stack of reports in the other.

"Thought you might need this," he said, stepping inside.

Haley eyed the coffee like it was salvation in a cup. "You know me too well, Steve," she muttered, reaching for it. "I need you to hold my calls while I go upstairs," she said, her voice laced with frustration.

Steve raised an eyebrow, immediately catching on. "Is this about the crab tweet?" he asked, his words tinged with amusement.

"Of course it is, Carl really outdid himself this time." she replied, letting out a sigh.

Steve chuckled, but the tension in Haley's posture didn't go unnoticed. "Good luck," he offered, still grinning as she stood up from her desk.

"Thanks," she said, offering a weary smile in return. With a final glance back at Steve, she pushed open the door and headed toward the elevator, bracing herself for what was to come.

The ride upstairs felt longer than usual, the weight of the impending conversation pressing down on her. Carl's ill-fated tweet had blown up far beyond what she expected, and now, she was on damage control, again. Just another fire to put out. She tried to steel herself, though her nerves were starting to fray. She took a big gulp of the coffee as she stepped off the elevator. What was it like to drink coffee slowly from a mug instead of a disposable cup, without a care in the world?

As she reached the top floor, the atmosphere shifted. Outside the imposing CEO office of Mega NRG Drink, Lauren, the CEO's assistant, sat behind her desk. With impeccably styled hair and an endless enthusiasm for office drama, Lauren looked up as Haley approached.

"You know the drill, Haley. Check in first, spill the tea second," Lauren said, leaning forward with a conspiratorial grin. "But seriously, does Carl really have crabs? Because the internet needs to know."

Haley groaned, dropping her bag onto the counter. "No, he doesn't have crabs. Just a lazy pun on his part," she muttered, shaking her head. "Carl really outdid himself this time. Years of social climbing, an Ivy League education, and now I'm dealing with the crab tweet."

Lauren let out a laugh so loud it turned a few heads. "Oh, honey, it's iconic."

"Glad you're enjoying the fallout," Haley muttered, massaging her temples. "Meanwhile, I'm trying to figure out how to spin this into something that doesn't tank our reputation."

Lauren leaned in, lowering her voice like she was about to share a state secret. "Between you and me, I think Carl's a genius. Crabs are trending now! I saw a TikTok about them taking over the world, and honestly? I'd let them."

Haley shot her a look. "Fantastic. Let me pitch that to the board—'crabocalypse branding: the future of energy drinks.' I'm sure they'll love it."

Lauren smirked, utterly unfazed.

Haley shook her head, stifling a laugh. "Thanks for the support, Lauren. I'm going to need it."

"Anytime, babe," Lauren called after her as she headed for Eric's office. "Oh, and if you need help with the apology tweet, I'm your girl. Just make sure it's claw-some!"

"Thanks, Lauren." Haley's phone suddenly came to life, buzzing insistently in her hand. With a sigh, she glanced down. "Sorry, Charlie. Not right now," she muttered under her breath, declining the call with a quick swipe of her finger. The last thing she needed was a conversation with her brother, there was no room for distractions. She tucked her phone back into her pocket and straightened her posture.

With another deep breath, Haley made her way toward the heavy wooden door. Time to face the music, she thought as she knocked softly, pushed it open, and stepped inside, preparing herself for whatever fallout was waiting for her.

Eric, with his tousled hair, backwards cap, and impeccably groomed stubble, was the picture of a reformed frat boy trying to adapt to a new corporate world. His designer hoodie and faded jeans whispered "laid-back," but the energy drink logo on his mug and the motivational posters on the wall—phrases like "Grind Harder" and "Rise & Hustle"—hinted at his past life. Now in his mid-thirties, he'd traded in keg parties for kombucha and was making a real effort to talk about "mindful management" and "cultural sensitivity," often sprinkling his sentences with buzzwords he'd picked up from leadership podcasts. Much of this shift had more than a little to do with his new girlfriend, Brooke—a fierce advocate for all things ethical and sustainable, who was on a mission to refine Eric into someone who could fit in with this new generation.

As Haley entered, she found him behind his desk, engrossed in a phone conversation. He leaned against the edge of the desk, one hand propping him up while the other held his phone to his ear. Spotting her, he gave her a relaxed grin, holding up a finger as if to say "just one sec."

"Alright, man. Yeah, totally. Sounds good. Alright, later!" Eric wrapped up his call with a grin, finally turning his attention to Haley.

"What's up, Haley?" He greeted her with a friendly smile, the unmistakable bro energy still shining through.

"Eric, I just want to assure you that Carl has been let go. We've deleted the tweet, and we have a team in place fielding complaints," Haley stated, all business, her tone serious.

Eric furrowed his brows, clearly confused. "Oh, okay, cool. Who's Carl?"

Haley blinked, her patience unwavering. "Carl, the social media guy? The one who sent out that offensive tweet yesterday?"

"Offensive? Really?" Eric's surprise was genuine. "The tweet about having crabs? That was hilarious. That wasn't us?"

"Nope," Haley confirmed, shaking her head. "Not us."

"Ah, bummer," Eric shrugged. "I thought you came up with that one, Hales. No worries, though. That's not why I called you up here."

Haley sighed, pushing the whole social media crisis out of her mind for the moment. "Oh, great, so what's up?"

Eric leaned forward, his tone shifting as he got to the real reason behind the meeting. "As you know, we've got several grocery chains wanting to buy the company."

Haley nodded, her determination reignited. "I'm ready to help however I can."

"That's my girl!" Eric exclaimed, then quickly backtracked. "Sorry, not my girl, of course. You know what I mean."

Haley cracked a small smile, amused at his attempt to be politically correct. "I do."

"Anyway," Eric continued, leaning back in his chair, "I'm taking a few of the guys to Arizona for a retreat, and I need a baller presentation to show them. You've got shares in this company, so the better the pitch, the bigger your check'll be."

Haley's confidence was palpable. "I got this, Eric. Consider it done."

"I know you do. High five!" Eric said, extending his hand, his enthusiasm practically overflowing.

With a quick grin, Haley met his high-five with a satisfying slap, the energy between them buzzing with excitement. She walked out of the office feeling a surge of determination. Time to tackle this next challenge head-on.

Chapter 2

Charles sat at the worn wooden desk, the flannel shirt he wore fitting the rustic charm of the room. He hung up the phone with a heavy sigh, staring at it for a moment before turning to Kate, who leaned casually against the wall across the room, her eyes fixed on him.

"How many times have you called?" Kate asked, her tone tinged with frustration.

Charles shook his head, glancing back at her. "She's busy. She'll call back."

Kate crossed her arms, her impatience evident. "Does she know how important this is? I think we should run the numbers again or reach out to Cedar Creek Bank."

Charles leaned back in his chair, rubbing his temples. "I've already got a meeting with Cedar Creek next week. But running the numbers won't change the fact that we're stretched too thin."

Before the conversation could go any further, Meemaw entered from the kitchen, her presence as commanding as ever. Her hands, slightly wrinkled but strong, rested on her hips, and her calm but firm voice broke the tension in the room.

"We need Haley's help," Meemaw said, her words laced with quiet confidence. "I don't know why, but my gut tells me she needs to be here."

Charles nodded slightly, knowing better than to argue with Meemaw's instincts. She always had a way of sensing things before they unfolded. "I've learned not to doubt your gut," he said. "I'll keep trying her."

Kate pushed herself off the wall with a frustrated sigh. "Let's hope she answers the phone one of these days." She shot Charles a pointed look before leaving the office, her footsteps echoing down the hall.

Once they were alone, Charles leaned forward, his voice quieter, more hesitant. "Meemaw, I know this isn't what you want to hear, but maybe it's time to think about selling. There's already an offer, and the money would be enough for you to retire comfortably. We could settle things."

Meemaw's expression hardened, her eyes narrowing with determination. "You don't retire from something you love. This ranch has been in our family for generations. We survived the Depression, the 80s, and every storm in between. We'll get through this, too."

Charles hesitated, his concern for Meemaw evident. He had always admired her strength, but this time felt different. "Let's not put too much stock in Haley," he said softly, careful not to push too hard. "She's got her own life, her own battles. I don't want you to get hurt waiting for her to swoop in and save the day."

Meemaw's expression softened, but her resolve remained. "She's family, Charles. She'll come through. I'm not going to let my bad decision be passed onto you two. I'll make this right."

Charles leaned back, studying the lines on her face that had been carved by years of hard work and sacrifice. His gaze shifted momentarily to the window, where he could see the old cottage Kate lived in, the original building A.B. Hollis had constructed when he had just four acres to his name. A.B. couldn't read or write, so when he signed the land documents—papers Meemaw still kept tucked away in her cedar chest—he signed with an X.

Charles had always marveled at A.B.'s shrewdness. Despite being "poor as dirt" back then, A.B. saved every penny he could, slowly buying up land. When the Great Depression hit, and neighbors around him lost everything, A.B. swooped in and bought their parcels, eventually amassing the 100 acres they now called Hollis Hills Ranch.

Charles's thoughts drifted to the years after A.B.'s time, when Pawpaw and his father had rebuilt the old house and converted it into living quarters for the ranch hands. The family had thrived for a time, selling off the tobacco rights in the 1970s and transitioning into raising horses, cows, and chickens. But then Pawpaw got cancer, and everything changed.

The savings they had worked so hard to build dwindled, drained by mounting medical bills. They'd had no choice but to mortgage the ranch to cover the costs, a decision that had kept Pawpaw with them a little longer but left the family in a precarious financial position.

For a brief moment, the weight of their situation hung in the air. Neither of them spoke, but the unspoken bond between them was stronger than any words could express. They both knew that this ranch wasn't just land or a business—it was a part of their family's soul, and they would fight for it as long as they could.

As Charles picked up his phone to try Haley once more, he couldn't shake the feeling that time was running out, and the weight of that reality settled in his chest.

Chapter 3

Kate paced up and down the barn, her boots crunching on the dirt floor, the sound echoing the intensity of her rising frustration. She muttered to herself, words spilling out in a heated rant, her voice mingling with the faint rustle of hay and the occasional snort of a restless horse."Haley is so selfish! That's all it is. She doesn't think about anyone but herself. She's off with her big city, fancy job, acting like she's too good for this place. Meanwhile, Charles is running himself ragged. I've been here almost three years now and still haven't even met her! She doesn't visit, she doesn't call... She just doesn't care!"

Kate came to an abrupt stop, her gaze falling on Louie, her horse, who stood quietly in his stall, chewing on hay without a care in the world. His large, calm eyes locked onto hers, steady and unbothered by the noise she'd been making.

Kate let out a sharp sigh, dragging a hand through her hair. "And... I'm talking to a horse." Her voice cracked with frustration as the weight of her own words hit her. She shook her head, the absurdity of it all making her pace even faster, the tension radiating off her in waves.

With a heavy sigh, she made her way over to Louie's stall, resting her hand on his mane. He was a good listener—always had been. Kate leaned her forehead against his, closing her eyes for a moment as if in search of comfort, finding solace in the warmth of his presence. "At least you're always here," she whispered, the frustration in her voice giving way to quiet sadness.

Louie nuzzled her gently, his breath warm against her cheek, and for a moment, Kate let herself feel the small bit of peace that came with this quiet, unspoken connection.

"You know," she murmured, still resting against him, "maybe Haley doesn't care. Or maybe she does, but she's just too wrapped up in her world to see what's happening here. Either way, something has to give."

She stayed like that for a while, leaning against Louie, letting the quiet barn and the steady rhythm of his breathing calm her down. But deep inside, the uncertainty still gnawed at her. Haley wasn't just some distant relative; she was the one everyone kept waiting on, the one who might have the answer to all their problems. Still, Kate couldn't shake her doubts. What if Haley never came? Or worse, what if Haley didn't have the answers? Then what? They'd be left to figure it all out on their own.

The thought lingered as Kate pulled back, giving Louie one final pat. She knew that, no matter what, she had to be prepared for whatever came next—whether Haley showed up or not.

Chapter 4

Haley stepped up to the host stand at the upscale restaurant, her heels clicking softly against the polished marble floor. The soft hum of low conversation and the clinking of silverware on fine china surrounded her. The dining room was dimly lit, with flickering candlelight casting warm, golden glows over the tables draped in crisp white linen. She glanced nervously around, her eyes darting to the sleek decor—modern art on the walls, a grand chandelier hanging over the center of the room, and an impressive wine rack that seemed more like a display of status than function.

The host, dressed in a perfectly tailored suit that screamed indifference, finally sauntered back to his post. His cool demeanor matched the restaurant's aura of exclusivity, and he barely glanced at Haley as he addressed her.

"Name?" he asked, his voice flat, like he'd repeated this process a thousand times and had long since stopped caring.

"It should be under Haley," she replied, offering a tight smile, trying to ignore the knot of nerves twisting in her stomach. She could feel the weight of the room, the glances of other patrons sizing her up, though she tried to shake it off.

The host scanned his list with deliberate slowness. "Two?"

"Yes," Haley confirmed with a nod.

He still didn't bother to meet her eyes. "Is the rest of your party here?"

"Um, no. I'm a bit early. Online date. First one in a while." She chuckled awkwardly, her laugh sounding hollow even to herself. "I'm kind of nervous."

The host's face remained a blank canvas, but his tone oozed condescension. "Oh. Hmm."

Haley hesitated, self-consciousness washing over her in waves. "Is that... sad? Do I seem too eager or desperate?"

"Kind of," the host replied bluntly, his words as sharp as a knife. "I'll show you to your table."

She blinked, startled by the casual cruelty, but followed him anyway, the heels of her boots sinking into the plush carpet as they weaved through the elegant restaurant. He led her to a small table tucked near the bar, away from the more desirable, central spots with views of the city skyline. The low hum of conversation felt louder here, the bar's hustle and bustle buzzing in the background.

"We're kind of far from the door," she joked weakly, trying to break the tension. "What if I need to make a quick escape?"

The host didn't even flinch. "Hilarious," he said, deadpan. "Why don't you sit at the bar until your party gets here?"

With that, he turned and walked away, leaving Haley feeling small and out of place in the elegant surroundings. She sighed, sliding onto a barstool, the polished leather seat cool under her. She signaled the bartender with a small wave and said, "Chardonnay, please."

As she pulled out her phone, the soft glow of the screen illuminated her face. A flood of notifications appeared—

100 unread emails, countless messages. The chaos of her life, laid out in digital form.

Great, she thought, tapping open her inbox. But before she could read even the first message, her phone buzzed again —an incoming call.

It was Charles.

Haley sighed deeply, her shoulders slumping as she swiped to answer. "Charles, I am on my first date in, like, a year. I cannot talk right now. I'll call you later."

She ended the call and placed her phone face down on the bar, staring blankly at the dimly lit room. The date hadn't even started, but the tension between her life in San Francisco and the pull of her family's ranch weighed on her like an anchor.

As she sipped the wine in front of her, Haley sat up a little straighter, trying to compose herself. The truth was, whether Haley liked it or not, her life was always going to be a balancing act between the glittering world she'd built in the city and the deep-rooted ties to the ranch that kept pulling her back.

She let out a long sigh, tucking a piece of hair behind her ear as she noticed the host leading someone towards her. The woman approaching looked like she had stepped straight out of a "Blake Lively hipster fever dream"—young, stylish, and effortlessly cool. A wide-brimmed hat perched atop her tousled, beachy waves, while oversized geometric accessories completed the look, giving her an air of someone who could seamlessly transition from a music festival to an upscale restaurant without missing a beat.

"Oh-my-gosh-hi! You must be Haley!" the woman said, her voice bubbling with enthusiasm. She swooped in for a half-hearted millennial embrace, her arms barely touching Haley's shoulders before retreating.

Haley managed a polite smile. "Hi, it's nice to meet you."

Masonry, as Haley knew her from the dating app, pulled back slightly, her gaze quickly scanning Haley, sizing her up like a fashion critic. "Oh wow, your energy is just so great. Are you a Leo?"

"Pisces," Haley replied, unsure where this conversation was going. "And thank you."

Masonry stared at her for a moment, unblinking, her eyes wide as if she were trying to read Haley's soul. "Pisces, yes, I see it now. My energy reading has been so off this week. Don't you just hate that? What kind of lesbian am I if I can't sense your sign right away? It's like, how are we even supposed to function? Ugh, this solstice has been CRAZY."

Haley stifled a laugh, glancing down at her wine glass. "Yeah, well, I'm clearly not winning any 'Good Lesbian' awards either. I didn't even know the solstice was happening."

Masonry gasped, looking genuinely horrified. "How could you not know?! It's like... the moment for resetting your energy."

Haley agreed awkwardly, trying to keep up with the rapid-fire conversation. "So, Masonry—that's such a unique name..."

"Thank you!" Masonry beamed, clearly pleased with the compliment. "Yeah, I gave it to myself during a naming ceremony in Chile."

"A naming ceremony?" Haley echoed, trying to hide her confusion.

Masonry nodded enthusiastically, launching into the story. "Yeah, I was there setting my intentions for the new year, feeling all this weird burden, you know? My metaphysical adviser, Amy, was like, 'You cannot thrive in this world under the narcissistic shroud of your parental-given name.' So, I went to this butterfly meditation yurt, released it, and accepted my new name."

Haley blinked, trying to wrap her mind around the idea. "That sounds... unbelievable. And how did you choose 'Masonry'?"

"I didn't choose it. The universe did. I just received it," Masonry said, her tone full of reverence, as though this was the most obvious thing in the world.

"Of course," Haley nodded along, pretending it made sense. "So, what do you do?"

Masonry gave her a puzzled look. "Well, I exist..."

"No, I mean for work. Like, a job?" Haley clarified, feeling the conversation slipping away from her.

"Oh," Masonry replied with a soft laugh, as though the idea of work was quaint. "I'm a student."

"Cool. Where?" Haley asked, trying to latch onto something tangible.

Masonry gestured broadly, her hand sweeping across the restaurant. "Here."

Haley frowned. "The restaurant? Or the Haight?"

Masonry's eyes widened, as if the answer was glaringly obvious. "The world, of course."

"Oh." Haley paused, trying to make sense of the reply. "Does that... pay well?" she asked, half-joking.

"Money is a construct," Masonry replied, her tone shifting to something almost philosophical. "But if I had to measure the value of my worth, yes, it does. I have over two million followers on Snapback, and I make about $200k a year from that."

Haley nearly choked on her water. "Seriously?"

"Yeah, you should follow me if you don't already!" Masonry said casually, as if it were the most normal thing in the world. Then she tilted her head, her eyes narrowing slightly. "So, Haley, what do you do?"

"I'm the Vice President of Operations at Mega NRG Drink," Haley said, falling into her professional rhythm.

Masonry's expression remained flat, unimpressed. "Hmm. But what do you do?"

Haley blinked, confused. "I manage corporate relationships, branding, marketing..."

"Right. But what do you do?" Masonry repeated, as if Haley hadn't answered the question.

Haley hesitated, unsure how to respond. "I like hiking...?"

24 | . CHRISTMAS AT THE RANCH

Masonry leaned in closer, her voice suddenly taking on a serious, almost intense tone. "Haley, may I share my truth with you?"

For a moment, Haley thought Masonry might be leaning in for a kiss. Wait, is this happening? Am I ready for this kiss? The sudden closeness caught her off guard, and her thoughts spiraled. What if I misread this? What if I didn't? Her heart skipped a beat, and she tried to compose herself, willing her voice to sound steady as she nodded. "Sure."

Masonry took a deep breath, as though what she was about to say carried immense weight. "I am very much connecting with you on a human level, but not on a spiritual level. And not at all on a physical level."

Haley blinked, unsure how to react. "Oh. Okay."

With your permission, of course, I would like to leave this interaction. Would you release me so we can both continue our journeys? But, like, separately?" Masonry asked, her tone full of sincerity.

"Yes," Haley replied, relieved but still trying to process the bizarre turn of events. Release her? What does that even mean? The whole interaction left Haley feeling bewildered, as if she had stepped into some kind of philosophical improv exercise she hadn't agreed to join.

"Thank you. I am grateful for what I've learned from you. Good journey," Masonry said, smiling warmly, as though their encounter had been deeply meaningful. Haley managed a nod, still too stunned to respond, as Masonry turned and walked away.

"Good journey?" Haley repeated, confused.

"Exactly," Masonry said with a knowing nod. "Oh, and don't forget to follow me on Snapback! I'm doing a Chakra bracelet giveaway tomorrow!"

With that, Masonry performed a sweeping gesture as if cleansing her aura, then turned and left, her hat bouncing slightly as she walked away.

Haley sat back in her chair, staring blankly at the empty spot where Masonry had just stood. She took a deep breath, trying to process the whirlwind of absurdity that had unfolded in the last thirty minutes.

That... was a disaster, she thought, feeling a dull ache of secondhand embarrassment wash over her. It wasn't just that the date had been bad—it was that it had been bizarre, surreal even. From the moment Masonry had asked if she was a Leo to the "truth-sharing" about their mismatched energies, it felt like Haley had stepped into some sort of alternate reality where nothing made sense.

She glanced at the wineglass in front of her, half-tempted to finish it in one gulp just to dull the edges of her confusion. Is this what dating had become? Or was this just my luck? Haley couldn't remember the last time she'd been on a date that wasn't, at best, awkward and at worst, utterly painful. But this? This took the cake.

The whole thing was almost comical. A butterfly meditation yurt? She stifled a laugh. She could already picture herself telling this story to her friends, but somehow, in the moment, it wasn't funny. It was exhausting. Haley felt deflated, like she'd invested time and energy into something that had never stood a chance.

I. CHRISTMAS AT THE RANCH

Leaning back in her chair, she let out a long sigh. She'd been hoping that, after a year of no dating, tonight would be a fresh start—a step toward something real, something meaningful. Instead, it had been a crash course in why she hated online dating in the first place. I could've just stayed at home, ordered takeout, and binged a show. That would've been more productive.

She rubbed her temples, feeling the tension creep into her head. At least Masonry had given her an out. And maybe, in some way, that was a small victory—escaping this weird encounter without too much damage to her own energy.

Before she could dwell on the absurdity any longer, her phone buzzed from her purse, pulling her from her thoughts. She grabbed it and saw Charles's name flashing on the screen.

Haley waved down a waiter for another drink, her irritation evident in the tightness of her voice. As the waiter nodded and walked off, she pressed the phone harder to her ear. "Charles, honestly..."

"Please, don't hang up," Charles said quickly, his tone urgent.

Sensing the seriousness in his voice, Haley's expression softened. She leaned back in her chair, the tension slowly creeping in. "Oh my god, is everything okay? Is Meemaw okay? You're supposed to text 911 if—"

"She's fine. Kind of," Charles interrupted, his voice wavering. "I mean, she really wants you home, and... we need to talk about the ranch."

"The ranch?" Haley felt a knot form in her stomach. She sat up straighter, eyes narrowing. "What about it?"

"It's in trouble, Haley. Things are getting bad."

Haley's brows furrowed in disbelief. "How is that possible? Isn't superwoman ranch hand Kate there to save everyone?" The sarcasm dripped from her voice.

Charles sighed heavily on the other end. "I don't want to get into details over the phone. Please, just come home for a little while. We need your help."

"I don't know, Charles." Haley's eyes darted around the restaurant, the lively atmosphere suddenly feeling suffocating. "I have this big project—"

"Haley, listen," Charles cut in, his voice firm but pleading. "Meemaw refinanced to cover Pawpaw's hospital expenses, and... it's caught up with us."

Haley's heart sank, her breath catching in her throat. "Oh no."

"Yeah," Charles continued. "I've been trying to work with the bank, but we're running out of options."

Haley's fingers tightened around her phone, her mind racing. "This is such bad timing. I have a huge presentation coming up. I can't just—"

"We have WiFi," Charles said, desperation creeping into his voice. "You can work from here. But please, Haley, I'm begging you. You haven't been back in a while, and if we can't figure this out... we'll have to sell."

Haley fell silent, the gravity of the situation settling over her like a heavy blanket. She looked out the window, the lights of San Francisco flickering in the distance. The ranch... gone? She couldn't even imagine it.

"Okay, I see," Haley finally replied, her tone flat. "The guilt trip."

"You always loved Christmas at the ranch," Charles added, his voice softening, trying to pull at her heartstrings.

"It'll be a massive, massive inconvenience for me..." Haley sighed, still clinging to some resistance, but knowing the outcome was inevitable.

"So... you're coming?" Charles asked, a flicker of hope in his voice.

Haley rolled her eyes but couldn't help the smile tugging at her lips. "I'll have to work remotely, of course."

"You're coming," Charles said again. Almost as if he didn't believe what he was hearing.

"Yes," Haley finally agreed, feeling the weight of her decision settle over her. "I'll come."

"Okay. Thank you," Charles breathed, his relief palpable.

"You're welcome," Haley muttered before hanging up the phone.

She stared down at the table, her drink untouched, the noise of the restaurant fading into the background. The weight of the conversation hung heavy in the air. The ranch, Meemaw, the debt—it all collided with her life in the city. How did it get this bad? she thought, her chest tightening. This trip home wasn't just a minor inconvenience; it was a return to a life she thought she'd left behind.

Chapter 5

Kate sat on the porch, the wood creaking beneath her chair the only sound cutting through the quiet, star-filled night. The sky above stretched endlessly, each star shimmering like a tiny promise, though none seemed to be meant for her. The gentle breeze carried the faint scent of hay and pine; the occasional rustle from the barn a reminder the horses were inside, peacefully resting after a long day.

With a sigh, she absently picked up her phone and opened a dating app. The screen glowed in the darkness, casting a faint blue light on her face as she swiped through a few profiles. The same faces she'd seen countless times before. The app quickly flashed its dreaded message: "No one new near you." She stared at the words for a moment, the isolation of it sinking deeper than she cared to admit. With a heavy sigh, she closed the app and slipped the phone back into her pocket.

She stood up, her boots scraping against the wooden floor as she made her way to the edge of the porch. She leaned against one of the old posts, her hands gripping the rough wood as her eyes locked on the expansive sky. The stars, bright and plentiful, felt distant—just like everything else in her life lately. Out here, in the middle of nowhere, the universe felt both vast and impossibly lonely.

"The biggest place with the least amount of people," she muttered to herself. "Never gonna meet anyone new out here. And even if I did, what would I say? 'Hi, I only talk to horses and occasionally myself.' Yeah, that's a winning conversation starter." She shook her head, chuckling softly at the absurdity of it all.

I. CHRISTMAS AT THE RANCH

The horses had become her world—her confidants, her company in the endless solitude of the ranch. Their steady presence grounded her; they were her only companions in the quiet, empty hours, and she poured herself into caring for them. In the mornings, she found solace in their soft whinnies, their warmth beside her, the gentle press of a muzzle against her hand. Yet, as much as she loved them, there was a loneliness that gnawed at her, a need they could never quite fill. Horses were loyal, sure, but their loyalty was simple, undemanding. They couldn't talk back, couldn't share the burdens of the heart or offer insight when her thoughts spiraled.

Deep down, Kate craved human connection—someone who could read her silences, understand the language of her heart without words.

Looking up at the stars, she felt the familiar pang of solitude, a hollow ache in her chest. She wanted to know someone else was out there, sharing her world, someone who could see her and maybe—just maybe—fill the silence that even her beloved animals couldn't touch.

With quiet resolve, she spoke to the universe, her voice barely a whisper. "Alright, universe. I don't want to get all Mariah Carey on you, but... whoever's out there, the only thing I want for Christmas this year is someone to share it with. Someone to talk to who isn't covered in hay or, you know, four-legged." She paused, chuckling softly at herself. "That's just between us, okay? I'm not saying I'm desperate, but... well, I just asked Santa Claus for a girlfriend. So, yeah. I'm officially losing it."

She let out a long breath, her words disappearing in the cool, night air. There was a certain sadness to it, the kind that comes from longing for something you're not sure even exists. But for a brief moment, she allowed herself to hope that maybe, just maybe, the universe had heard her.

With a small, rueful smile, Kate stepped off the porch, her boots crunching softly on the gravel path as she made her way back toward her little house on the ranch. The moonlight illuminated her path, casting long shadows as she walked, lost in thought.

Unbeknownst to Kate, Meemaw stood just off to the side of the porch, hidden in the shadows, her wise, old eyes gazing up at the same sky. She had heard Kate's quiet plea to the universe, her heart softening at the vulnerability in her words. Meemaw smiled softly to herself, shaking her head as if to say, "Patience, Kate. Things have a way of working out."

Without a word, Meemaw turned and made her way back toward the main house, her thoughts lingering on her granddaughter. She knew Hailey wouldn't let the family down. She would arrive soon. Kate didn't realize it, but she wasn't as alone as she felt. And maybe, just maybe, this Christmas, the universe would have something special in store for her.

As Meemaw's figure faded into the dim light of the house, silence settled over the ranch once more. The stars continued their quiet vigil above, casting a gentle glow across the fields. In that moment, the night seemed to hold its breath, as if waiting for the promise of change.

As Kate entered her small house, she glanced around the quiet room filled with the familiar comforts of home—shelves lined with books, a worn armchair by the fire, and a framed photo of her and Meemaw from last Christmas. The ranch was everything to her, but the weight of its solitude was heavier tonight than it had been in a long time.

She kicked off her boots and sank into the chair, staring into the fire as it crackled softly, the flames flickering like distant stars. Her mind began to drift, and she imagined what it would be like to have someone there, sitting beside her, holding her hand. Someone to share the warmth and the quiet moments, the simple joys of ranch life, and perhaps even the life they could build together. The thought lingered, filling the empty room with a quiet sense of longing and possibility.

Chapter 6

Haley stepped into her apartment, kicking the door shut behind her with more force than necessary. The familiar click of the lock echoed through the quiet space, but tonight, the calm wasn't comforting. It felt heavy. She tossed her keys onto the counter and slumped against the back of the door, eyes closed, replaying the mess of a night.

The date had been a disaster—there was no other way to put it. Between Masonry's solstice energy readings, at least that's what she assumed it had been and her bizarre exit, Haley could barely wrap her head around what had just happened.

But the date wasn't what weighed on her now. No, the real pressure came from the conversation with Charles. The ranch. Meemaw. The fact that she had promised to go back — promised to help save the one place that had always felt like home but also a world she'd left behind for a reason. Now she was going back, whether she was ready or not.

Haley pushed off the door and walked into her living room, dropping onto the couch. The soft hum of city traffic outside her window barely registered as she buried her face in her hands.

"What have I done?" she muttered, her voice muffled by her palms. She wasn't just committing to a long weekend trip. She was committing to... what exactly? Saving the ranch? Being the hero for Meemaw and Charles? She wasn't sure where to even begin, and the thought of juggling that alongside the massive project she'd eagerly taken on at work made her feel as if she were teetering on the edge of a cliff.

Oh God. Haley's mind raced, her thoughts colliding like speeding cars. The company was banking on her, and she wasn't about to let her team down, but how was she going to juggle both? She couldn't lose her job, but she couldn't let Meemaw lose the ranch either.

The idea of working remotely from the ranch seemed impossible. Sure, Charles said they had Wi-Fi, but Haley could already imagine the spotty connections, the frustration of trying to manage corporate meetings while dodging hay bales and cowbells. The vision made her laugh for a second before reality settled back in, heavy as ever.

And then there was Kate. Haley had never met her, but she already felt a simmering resentment toward the ranch hand Charles and Meemaw couldn't seem to stop praising. Kate, who was always talked about like she could do no wrong, who seemed to have slipped seamlessly into the space Haley had once occupied. Even though Haley had chosen to stay away, it stung to think that someone else had filled the gap so perfectly. As if she'd been replaced without anyone even noticing.

She groaned, sinking deeper into the couch. "I'm going to lose my mind."

For as long as she could remember, the ranch had been Meemaw's pride and joy. It wasn't just land—it was the heart of their family. The thought of it being sold, gone forever, twisted something deep in Haley's chest that cut like a knife. Meemaw had been strong for so long, carrying the weight of everything. Haley didn't know how to tell her no. She didn't want to say no. But the pressure felt like it was crushing her from all sides.

"I can't do this," Haley whispered, though she knew the decision had already been made. She had to go.

She took a deep breath, pushing herself up from the couch. Tomorrow, she'd pack, face her responsibilities, and head back to the ranch. But tonight, she needed a moment to process. To let the fear, the frustration, and the overwhelming sense of responsibility wash over her.

She headed to the kitchen and poured herself a glass of wine, gripping the stem tightly as she stared out the window at the city lights. It felt like the calm before the storm, but she knew she'd have to face it head-on, whether she was ready or not.

For Meemaw. For the ranch. And maybe, if she could figure out how to manage everything, for herself.

Chapter 7

Haley stood in her office, surrounded by the clutter of last-minute planning. Her laptop was open on the desk, tabs of airline schedules and work emails flashing across the screen. Papers were scattered everywhere, like a whirlwind had swept through. She was packing her work life into a neat little box before heading back to the ranch—a place that felt anything but neat.

Steve strolled in, a steaming cup of tea in his hand, watching her with an amused smirk.

"Okay, lady, calm it right down," he teased, leaning casually against the doorframe. "You're not leaving the country."

Haley paused, trying to collect herself, but her fingers still drummed against the desk. "Yes, you're right," she exhaled, her voice a little shaky. "Deep breaths." She picked up her phone and stared at it. "I have to go tell Eric... right after he dumped this massive presentation on me."

Steve shrugged, a grin tugging at the corner of his mouth. "You could do this with your eyes closed, Haley. You're going to crush it."

"Thanks," she replied, a small, grateful smile tugging at her lips. Steve's steady presence was like a lifeline in moments like these, grounding her when everything else felt overwhelming. For a fleeting second, she wondered if she could convince him to come back with her—be her personal assistant in saving the ranch. But reality set back in as her eyes flicked to the paper in his hand. "Is that my itinerary?"

"Yes, ma'am," Steve handed it to her with a slight flourish, clearly enjoying himself. "You're all set to fly out."

Haley scanned the document, her eyes narrowing at the number of layovers. "Wait. How many connections do I have?"

Steve winced dramatically. "Sorry, that was the best I could do. Apparently, planes prefer landing on runways, not fields." He gave her a playful grin.

"Very funny," she muttered, but the joke eased some of her tension. "Wish me luck."

"Good luck!" Steve called after her as she grabbed her bag and headed for the door, already pulling herself into work mode for the next hurdle.

Morning light filtered through the wide office windows as Haley stepped off the elevator, her heels clicking softly on the polished floor. She moved with purpose, though a hint of tension clung to her shoulders, betraying her usual calm demeanor. As she approached Lauren's desk, she noticed the soft hum of conversation in the distance, the familiar rhythm of the office that usually soothed her, but today, it only heightened her unease.

Lauren sat behind her desk, phone pressed to her ear, her voice hushed. "I'm telling you, they're done. No couple photos in four months. Four. And she unfollowed him last week. That's basically the social media equivalent of a breakup announcement."

Haley cleared her throat gently, biting back a smile as she pulled herself back to the present.

Lauren glanced up, quickly ending the call with a whispered, "I'll get the full scoop later!" She set her phone down, her face lighting up with a warm, familiar smile. "Haley, please tell me you've got something better than the office breakup drama, because I'm running on rumors and caffeine over here."

"I need to see Eric," Haley said, the words spilling out with more urgency than she intended. She took a steadying breath, trying to maintain some semblance of control over the growing anxiety that gnawed at her.

Lauren paused, her brow furrowing slightly. "Eric's already gone. He left early this morning for Arizona, prepping for the big meetings."

Haley blinked, relieved. She hadn't expected him to leave so soon, but then again, Eric had always been the type to jump in headfirst. This made Haley feel better about leaving. Eric is remote and she will be too.

"I'm heading home for a family thing," she said, trying to keep her tone steady, though the weight of what lay ahead pressed heavily on her chest. "I'll be working remotely. My phone will be on, and I'll keep up with emails."

Lauren's expression softened, "Ok".

Haley offered a weak smile, appreciating the understanding. "Just make sure Eric knows I'll be out of the office, but everything will still get handled."

Lauren gave a reassuring nod. "I'll let him know. You'll be fine, Haley. You've got this."

The warmth in Lauren's voice soothed some of the tension knotted in Haley's shoulders, but as she turned to leave, that familiar weight settled back over her. The promise she'd made to Charles, the uncertainty of what awaited her at the ranch—it all felt heavier now, pressing down on her with every step she took away from the office.

She paused at the door, glancing back at the familiar environment, then exhaled, steeling herself for what was to come. The ranch was calling her back, and whether she was ready or not, it was time to face it.

Chapter 8

The early morning light spilled through the open doors of the barn, casting long shadows across the packed dirt floor. Inside, the quiet sounds of horses shifting in their stalls and the soft clinks of metal as Kate packed up Louie's saddle mixed with the calm of the ranch waking up for the day. Meemaw was nearby, her weathered hands moving skillfully as she helped Kate prepare for the trip ahead. The two worked together in a comfortable, unspoken rhythm, one built over time with shared routines. There was no need for words—just the quiet understanding that comes from years of familiarity and trust.

For Kate, Meemaw had become more than just a mentor; she had become the mother figure she never knew she needed. After Kate made the difficult decision to distance herself from her own parents, she found refuge here on the ranch. Meemaw filled that aching void with her kindness, wisdom, and steady presence. Where Kate's relationship with her own mother had been strained and distant, Meemaw's warmth provided the love and guidance she had been missing for so long.

As they moved through the motions of packing and prepping, Kate couldn't help but feel a sense of gratitude. Meemaw's gentle instruction and unwavering support had been a lifeline, grounding her in a way she hadn't felt in years. It was as if they both knew that the work they were doing wasn't just about preparing for the trip—it was about something deeper, a bond that had grown between them, stronger with each passing season.

Kate tightened the last strap on Louie's saddle when the sound of boots crunching against the ground grabbed her attention as Charles walked in, his arms crossed over his chest with a questioning look on his face.

"Going somewhere?" he asked, eyeing the packed bags and the fully saddled horse.

Kate barely glanced up from her task. "Some hunters said there's a fence post broken down by the creek," she explained, checking Louie's bridle. "I'm going to take a look, and then I'll pick up some supplies."

Charles raised an eyebrow. "You can't do all that in one day."

Kate shrugged, lifting the reins as she prepared to lead Louie out of the barn. "I know," she said, her voice steady. "I'll set up camp and head back early in the morning."

Charles frowned, stepping closer. "You can't stay the night outside."

Kate smirked, finally looking up at him. "I do it all the time. Camping in the cold is one of my favorite things."

"I know," Charles said, his tone softening, "but there's a bad storm coming."

Kate rolled her eyes, her voice tinged with exasperation. "You really don't know how to read the weather, do you? The storm's coming in a few days. I'll have my phone, and I've got my fancy signal booster."

Charles wasn't convinced. "Please, just go to Fox Springs and stay at the lodge tonight."

42 | CHRISTMAS AT THE RANCH

Kate paused, eyeing him for a moment, as if weighing her options. "Would that get you off my case?"

Charles smiled, relieved. "Yes."

Kate sighed dramatically, shaking her head but giving in. "Okay, fine. I'll stay at the lodge. Just trying to save money, you know."

Meemaw, watching the exchange with a knowing smile, chuckled under her breath. The familiar banter between Kate and Charles was like a daily dance, both of them stubborn in their own ways but always looking out for each other.

Just then, the distant rumble of a truck echoed up the drive. The sound grew louder, and a massive pickup rolled into view, its engine grumbling as it came to a stop. They all turned to face the intrusion, their expressions instantly darkening.

"You've got to be kidding me," Charles muttered, his face tightening as the truck door swung open.

Meemaw's eyes narrowed into slits. "What is that vulture doing here?"

Bert, a man in his late fifties, wearing fancy jeans, a cowboy hat, and a smirk that made Meemaw's blood boil, stepped out of the driver's side. His son, Bert Jr., climbed out of the passenger seat, a younger, cockier version of his father with a swagger in his step.

"Good morning," Bert called out, his voice dripping with faux friendliness. "Heard y'all got a fence post broken down by the creek. Pretty generous of me to still want to buy this place, even when it's falling apart."

Before anyone could respond, Meemaw lunged forward, her face flushed with fury. "You slimy little—"

Charles quickly grabbed her arm, holding her back. "Easy, Meemaw."

She struggled for a moment, eyes blazing, before Charles managed to calm her down. "Get off my ranch!" she yelled, her voice sharp and unwavering.

Bert and his son, momentarily startled, took a step back, moving behind their truck for cover. Once they realized there was no real threat, they regained their composure, but the smirks were gone.

Charles, keeping his voice level, addressed them. "What can I do for you, Bert?"

Bert sidled around the truck, his hat tilted slightly as if trying to appear casual. "Thought I'd stop by and see if y'all needed help with that fence," he said, flashing a grin. "Just being neighborly."

Charles shook his head. "Actually, Kate was just packing up to go down and fix it. So, we're good."

Bert raised an eyebrow, clearly unimpressed. "Her? She's gonna fix a fence by herself?"

Before Kate could respond, Bert Jr. jumped in, gesturing to the nearby fences. "Don't worry, Kate. When I take over, I'll get you off ranch duty and put you in the kitchen where you can be more useful."

His laugh rang out, grating against the tension already thick in the air. Kate glared at him, her jaw tightening. "I'll pass," she muttered through clenched teeth.

Ignoring the insult, Bert stepped closer to Charles, lowering his voice slightly. "My offer ain't gonna be on the table forever, Charles. It's me or the bank."

Charles didn't flinch, keeping his tone calm but firm. "I can't do anything until my sister gets here, Bert. This is a family decision."

Bert's smirk returned. "Good. Hopefully, she can talk some sense into you."

Charles held his ground. "Is that all?"

"Yeah, that's all," Bert said with a shrug. He motioned for his son to follow, but before climbing back into his truck, he couldn't resist one last dig. "Kate, when y'all are done with the Christmas hayride, come on over and help with ours! Merry Christmas!"

Bert and his son laughed as they hopped back into the truck, peeling out in a cloud of dust.

Meemaw moved to stand beside Charles, watching the truck disappear into the distance.

"Thank God Haley's coming," Meemaw murmured. "Can't wait to see their faces when we tear up those contracts."

Later that morning, the sun climbed higher in the sky as Charles worked steadily, moving the fencing to guide the cows to fresh pasture. The field stretched wide around him, a familiar expanse of green dotted with the slow, deliberate movements of the herd. This work, though repetitive and physically demanding, was second nature by now. The soft clank of metal and the occasional lowing of cows were the only sounds that broke the silence.

Every step felt like a reminder of the endless tasks that came with ranch life, the constant maintenance, the daily grind. But for Charles, there was comfort in the rhythm The wide-open space offered a kind of peace, even with the ranch's financial troubles looming in the back of his mind. Out here, beneath the expansive blue sky, the burden of the ranch seemed to fade—if only for a moment.

He paused, wiping the sweat from his brow, and glanced up. In the distance, Kate was riding across the field, Louie's strong legs carrying her swiftly over the uneven terrain. Her figure was a blur against the backdrop of trees and hills, the wind whipping through her hair as she leaned forward, urging Louie to go faster. There was something freeing about watching her ride, a reminder of the simple joys that the ranch had always provided, even amidst the stress. That was why it was so important to do whatever it took to not lose the ranch. Not now. There was too much to lose.

Charles finished securing the last section of fencing, giving the post a final shove to make sure it held firm. He stood for a moment, hands on his hips, surveying the land around him. Kate had disappeared into the distance, and for a moment, all was still.

He glanced down at his hands, dirt-smudged and sporting a fresh scrape from when he'd fumbled the hammer earlier.

Thank God Haley's coming, he thought, echoing Meemaw's words from earlier. They needed her now more than ever.

Chapter 9

Kate walked toward the lodge's main office; her gear slung casually over her shoulder. She had already taken care of her horse, leading it to the lodge's stable and making sure it was settled with fresh hay and water before heading inside. The familiar sight of the main lodge greeted her; its rustic charm standing out against the cool night air. It was a place she knew well, a refuge from the long days on the ranch. Stepping into the cozy office, Kate was greeted by the soft glow of warm lights and the comforting scent of old wood and firewood burning in the fireplace. The space was simple but inviting, a welcome retreat from the cold outside. As she approached the front desk, Lucy, who was about the same age as Charles, looked up from her paperwork and smiled brightly.

"Well, hey, Kate! I thought I might be seeing you," Lucy said, her voice full of cheer. "Heard about that broken fence post down by the creek. Saved Ol' Louie a spot in the barn."

Kate gave a grateful nod, shifting the strap of her bag on her shoulder. "Thanks. I appreciate that, Lucy. I saw the apple you left for him. That was so sweet. How's Walter and the kids?"

"They're good," Lucy replied with an exaggerated sigh. "Driving me to my absolute wits' end, but good." She leaned forward with a wink. "You want your usual room?"

"That'd be great, thank you," Kate said, her voice warm with familiarity.

Lucy turned and reached for a key behind the desk, handing it over with a grin. "Alright, here's your key. And the HBO is working tonight!"

Kate chuckled, pocketing the key. "Oh, great. That'll keep me entertained. Thanks, Luce."

"Merry Christmas!" Lucy called after her as Kate turned to leave.

"Merry Christmas!" Kate replied, giving a quick wave before stepping back out into the crisp night air.

The lodge was quiet as Kate walked toward her room, the sky dark and clear above her, stars twinkling faintly. It was a peaceful contrast to the busy day she had left behind, a moment of quiet before she had to head back to the ranch the next morning.

***

Lucy was still behind the desk when the door creaked open a few minutes later, and Haley stumbled in, struggling with her roller bag. The cold air followed her inside, and the door slammed shut with a final thud as Haley fought to steady herself. Her breath came out in visible puffs as she tried to catch it, cheeks flushed from the biting cold.

"Need some help, hon?" Lucy asked, watching with barely concealed amusement as Haley awkwardly wrestled her luggage.

"No, no, it's fine," Haley replied, still out of breath. "I just need a bed. The name is Haley Hollis."

Lucy's eyes widened, her posture straightening as recognition dawned. "Oh my god. Haley? Charlie's sister?"

Haley blinked, slightly caught off guard by the excitement in Lucy's voice. "Yes, that's me."

"Well, I'll be!" Lucy exclaimed, her voice rising with enthusiasm. "It's me, Lucy Brunson! Well, Wyman now—I got married. Charlie and I dated for a while in high school!"

Haley's face lit up in recognition as she put the pieces together. "Lucy! Of course. How are you?"

"Oh, I'm great," Lucy replied, her hands flapping excitedly as she leaned over the counter. "Three kids and all that jazz. Moved up here to Fox Springs about ten years ago. What can I say? I'm a city girl at heart."

Haley's eyes flicked around the small, rural lodge. She raised an eyebrow, suppressing a smirk. "Yes. This certainly is a city... technically."

Lucy chuckled, clearly catching the teasing tone. "It has its charms, I guess. But what are you doing these days? I heard you went to Dart... something?"

"Dartmouth. Yes, I did," Haley replied, starting to explain. "Now I work in San Francisco at a—"

"Oh wow, that sounds amazing!" Lucy interrupted, her eyes widening with admiration. "I always wanted to go to California. The weather just seems like a dream come true. I bet you miss the warm weather when you visit, huh? No palm trees and movie stars up here! Although..." She paused, leaning in conspiratorially, "I did do a couple of commercials for the mattress outlet in town."

Haley blinked, surprised by the sudden shift. "Commercials?"

Lucy grinned wide, unable to resist. She began singing, "♪ You'll sleep like a baby, no ifs, ands, or maybes, at Bill's Mattress Emporium—prices so low, you'll snore! ♪"

Haley burst into laughter, her earlier exhaustion melting away. Lucy's enthusiasm was infectious, and the absurdity of the situation made the day's stresses feel distant, if only for a moment.

"Wow," Haley said, still chuckling. "Hollywood missed out on you, Lucy."

Lucy gave a mock bow. "Their loss, right? Now, let's get you checked in and settled before I break out the full jingle set."

"Sounds good." Haley grinned, feeling a strange sense of comfort in the warmth of this small-town encounter.

"Of course! Here you go," Lucy said, handing over the room key with a cheerful flourish. "I put you in the good room. Right next to the ice machine!"

Haley hesitated, unsure how to respond. "Oh. Thank you?"

"You're welcome!" Lucy said, oblivious to the awkwardness. "Enjoy your stay with us, and Merry Christmas!"

Haley nodded, her mind drifting to why she was even staying at the lodge in the first place. She had hoped to go straight to the ranch, but it had gotten too late for Charles to come and pick her up. The idea of making him drive all that way in the dark didn't sit right with her, and, truthfully, after the long trip, she wasn't ready for another round of conversations about the ranch. A night alone, even next to an ice machine, seemed like the best option.

With a polite nod, she turned and stepped back out into the freezing night. The cold hit her immediately, the icy air wrapping around her as she pulled her coat tighter and hurried toward her room. The warmth of the lodge and Lucy's enthusiastic chatter faded behind her, leaving only the sharp bite of winter and the heavy thoughts of what awaited her at the ranch tomorrow.

Haley trudged through the cold, her breath forming small clouds in the icy air as she made her way to her room. The lodge was exactly what she had expected—a Midwest motor lodge straight out of the 80s. The walls were adorned with cheesy, outdated landscape prints, and the green carpet had long since passed its prime. A floral bedspread lay across the bed, its bright colors a stark contrast to the drab décor around it, screaming of charm from another era.

As soon as she stepped into the room and dropped her bag by the door, her phone rang. She sighed, setting down her things and answering the call.

"Hey! Are you here?" Charles' voice came through the line, upbeat and familiar.

"Yeah, I just got to the lodge," Haley replied, sinking onto the bed, the floral comforter crinkling beneath her.

"Great! I've got an important meeting with the bank in Cedar Creek tomorrow morning," Charles continued. "I'm sending the Uber to pick you up in the morning."

Haley frowned. "The Uber?"

"Yeah, we only have one in town," Charles explained, as if it were the most normal thing in the world.

"Of course you do," Haley muttered, shaking her head. The idea of a single Uber serving the entire town was both amusing and a little disheartening.

Sitting there for a moment, she let the quiet settle in around her. The exhaustion of the day weighed heavily on her, but the familiar buzz of her responsibilities tugged at the back of her mind. She opened her laptop and, with a soft sigh, clicked into her presentation—the one she had started working on during the plane ride. The moment she started typing, the world around her faded, and soon she was in the zone, ideas pouring out as her fingers moved furiously across the keyboard.

For a brief time, the worries of the ranch, the lodge's outdated charm, and the long road ahead slipped into the background, replaced by the comforting rhythm of her work.

Chapter 10

Haley paced around the small room muttering to herself as a sudden epiphany struck. Without missing a beat, she rushed back to the desk, fingers flying across the keyboard to capture the idea before it slipped away. Her focus was sharp, her thoughts coming together in a way that felt almost electric.

Moments later, restless energy bubbling inside her, she dropped to the floor and knocked out a quick set of sit-ups. "Clear the head, keep the blood flowing," she mumbled before settling back in front of the screen, quickly picking up where she left off.

Her voice filled the empty room as she talked her way through the presentation, the sound of her typing almost rhythmic in the otherwise quiet lodge. Her fingers tapped furiously, her thoughts flowing seamlessly into sentences, paragraphs, slides.

Finally, with a flourish, she typed the last few words and leaned back, closing the laptop with a satisfied snap. She threw her arms up like a victorious athlete.

"And the crowd goes wild for the greatest presentation EVER!" Haley announced to no one, grinning. "We're all going to be rich!"

Feeling triumphant, she performed a quick, exaggerated touchdown dance before flopping onto the bed, her chest still buzzing with excitement. She grabbed her phone, ready for a distraction, and began scrolling through Snapback.

That was, until a promoted post from Masonry popped up, showcasing turquoise "intention boxes." Haley rolled her eyes. Of course.

With a sigh, she closed the app and let the phone drop onto the bed, the energy of her victory already beginning to fade.

"Let's see what the scene is like in the big city," Haley muttered, opening a dating app and swiping through the usual suspects.

The first profile to pop up was Lucy's. Haley snorted, raising an eyebrow. "Lucy?" she whispered with a smirk. "Scandalous."

She kept scrolling, passing profiles that ranged from the bizarre to the expected: women who had been divorced three times, couples looking to spice things up, and curious married girls testing the waters. Each one more uninspiring than the last, until her finger froze over Kate's profile. Her handle was "CowGrrl," and her photos showcased a life spent outdoors, exuding strength, confidence, and an undeniable sense of authenticity. The first picture was of Kate leaning casually against a weathered fence post, her cowboy hat tipped low over her brow, the vast, open ranch stretching out behind her like a scene from an old western.

Haley blinked, surprised. "Well, this is different," she muttered.

The second photo showed Kate mid-laugh, riding a horse with the kind of carefree joy that instantly made Haley smile. She could almost hear the laughter through the screen, and it made something flutter in her stomach. Another picture showed Kate standing next to an old tractor, dressed in well-worn jeans and boots, her face squinting slightly against the sun. Her hair was loose, her skin kissed by the day's work, and she had that confident, grounded look of someone who knew where they belonged.

Haley couldn't help but notice how Kate was totally giving off sexy cowgirl vibes. There was something magnetic about her in those pictures—the effortless confidence, the effortless strength. It was clear Kate wasn't posing or trying to impress anyone; she was just... herself. And that made Haley's heart skip a beat.

Intrigued, Haley scrolled to Kate's bio. It was short and sweet, but the words hooked her immediately:

"Horse lover. Seeking someone down-to-earth who loves adventure, quiet nights, and maybe even getting their hands dirty. Not afraid to spend days in the barn or under the stars."

"Whoa now," Haley whispered to herself, feeling a slight flush creep up her neck. Her interest was undeniably piqued. She sat up a little straighter, staring at the profile with newfound curiosity. Was she really getting turned on by a few photos? She shook her head, smiling to herself. "Hello, cowgirl," she murmured, her heart beating faster than it had in a long time.

***

Kate walked from the bathroom into her bedroom, her hair still damp from the shower. The cool air of the room felt refreshing on her skin as she grabbed her phone from the nightstand. With a lazy flick of her finger, she opened the dating app, already preparing herself for the usual parade of familiar, uninspiring faces.

The first profile to pop up was Lucy's. Kate chuckled softly to herself. "Oh, Lucy," she muttered, amused. "That's why you and Walter keep inviting me for drinks. Very progressive. But no." She swiped left with a grin, shaking her head.

She continued scrolling, flipping through the same profiles she'd seen a hundred times before—familiar faces from around town that never really sparked her interest. But then she paused, her thumb hovering over a new name and face. Joan.

Intrigued, Kate clicked into the profile.

"Hello, Joan," she whispered, raising an eyebrow as she scrolled through Joan's pictures. "Not married. No kids. And less than a mile away." She tapped on a photo of Joan hiking with a dog named Miles, a friendly-looking golden retriever, by her side.

"Cute dog," Kate murmured, a smile tugging at her lips. "Automatic swipe right."

As soon as she swiped, a notification popped up on her screen. It was a match.

"Whoa," Kate said, her eyebrows shooting up in surprise. "That's never happened so fast." She sat up in bed, her heart unexpectedly racing as she stared at her phone. She hesitated for a moment, her thumb hovering over the screen, before taking a deep breath. "You can do this," she whispered to herself, trying to shake off the nervous energy. With a quick tap, she typed out a message:

56 | . CHRISTMAS AT THE RANCH

Cowgrrl: Hi. I like your dog.

Kate winced slightly, reading the words back as the message sent. *That's what you went with?* she thought, shaking her head in disbelief. Dropping the phone into her lap, she leaned back against the pillows, already second-guessing herself.

A few rooms down the hall, Haley's phone buzzed with a new notification. Glancing at the screen, she read the message and a grin immediately spread across her face.

"Oh, hot cowgirl," she muttered with amusement, "I bet she can start a fire from nothing. With a playful smile, Haley typed back:

Joan: Thanks. What am I, chopped liver?

Kate's phone buzzed again, and this time, she couldn't help but laugh out loud. She shook her head at her own awkwardness before quickly typing a reply:

Cowgrrl: No, you're cute too. Sorry. I'm bad at this.

Haley chuckled, shaking her head as she read the message.

Joan: Everyone's bad at it. It's awkward.

She typed back. Then, after a brief pause and a moment of consideration, she added:

Joan: We seem to be relatively close. Maybe this would be better in person. Would you want to grab a drink?

Kate stared at the message, her heart pounding in her chest. "Oh wow, she's bold!" she said aloud, her fingers hovering over the keyboard.

Cowgrrl: I'd love to. The Wet Whistle is close. Want to meet there?

She typed, her nerves buzzing as she hit send.

Haley read the reply, a spark of excitement rushing through her.

Joan: That sounds lovely. 30 minutes?

She typed back, feeling a flush of anticipation spread through her whole body. As she hit send, her thoughts began to drift, imagining how the night could unfold. The idea of sitting across from hot Cowgrrl, feeling that magnetic pull between them, and maybe ending the night with a lingering, perfect kiss—it all made her heart race. It had been too long since she felt this kind of excitement, and the flutter in her stomach only grew stronger as she thought about what might happen next.

Kate's phone buzzed again, and this time the weight of the situation hit her. Her nerves kicked in hard, twisting her stomach into knots. She stared at the message, eyes wide. "What am I doing?" she muttered to herself, fingers trembling as she typed her reply.

Cowgrrl: Yes.

As soon as she hit send, she threw her phone down and leapt from the bed. "Oh my god, I have to get ready... I have nothing with me!" she groaned, rushing around the room in a panic.

She grabbed her toiletries bag, frantically pulling out deodorant and Chapstick, but it wasn't enough. Glancing at herself in the mirror, an idea struck. With a flash of inspiration, she grabbed a box of wooden matches, lit one, and quickly blew it out. Using the burnt edge, she carefully applied makeshift eyeliner, smiling triumphantly at her resourcefulness.

"Good enough," she whispered to herself, tossing the matchstick away and rushing to find something halfway decent to wear.

***

Kate strode into the bar, her cowgirl boots clicking confidently on the dirt and hay-strewn floor, each step exuding a natural swagger. Her movements were loose and self-assured, as if she owned the space the moment she walked in. The familiar creak of the wooden planks beneath her feet mixed with the soft twang of country music playing in the background. The warm glow of the bar lights highlighted the rustic charm of the place, but it was Kate who seemed to command all the attention, her presence magnetic in the quiet, easy way she carried herself.

At the bar, Haley sat waiting, a glass of wine in hand. As the door creaked open, she turned just in time to see Kate stride in, her gaze immediately locking on the woman walking toward her. Haley couldn't help but smile, charmed by the sight of this confident, beautiful woman.

"Joan?" Kate asked, her eyes fixed on Haley.

Haley's smile widened as she turned fully to face her. "Cowgirl," she greeted with a playful grin.

Kate returned the smile, though there was a hint of unexpected shyness in her eyes. "I don't usually say yes to someone so quickly," she admitted, her fingers lightly tapping the counter. "But I'm glad I did. I spend most of my time with animals... I can go days without seeing another person."

"Interesting," Haley replied, tilting her head.

Just then, the bartender appeared, wiping his hands on a rag as he approached, giving them a nod.

"Hi," Kate said, flashing him a smile. "Beer, please."

The bar had a sleepy, laid-back vibe, with only one other patron—an older man named Bob, sitting alone at a table, playing solitaire with a beer in hand. It felt like the kind of place where time slowed down.

Haley glanced around the quiet bar before turning her attention back to Kate. "So, days without seeing another person. What do you do for a living?"

Kate hesitated, her mind racing. *What do I say?* She wasn't ready to tell some stranger at a bar about her whole life. The ranch, the family troubles—it felt too personal, too real. Besides, she wasn't sure if Joan would understand. Kate wasn't looking for pity, and she didn't want to dive into the mess of the ranch on the first meeting. So, she leaned into something simpler, something that wasn't a lie, but wasn't the whole truth either.

"I work at a zoo," she said with a half-smile. *It's not technically untrue—I do work with animals... just not the ones people expect.* But the distance it put between her and the reality of her life made her feel a little safer. "What about you? What do you do?"

Haley raised an eyebrow, intrigued by the answer but sensing there was more to it. She took a sip of her wine and set the glass down. "I'm in corporate," she said lightly, leaving it vague. "Mostly branding and marketing. Not as exciting as working with animals, though."

Kate chuckled softly, brushing a loose strand of hair behind her ear. "I don't know about that. But it has its moments."

"My moments are boring meetings. PowerPoints and social media," Haley said with a shrug, swirling her wine glass absentmindedly.

Kate raised an eyebrow, intrigued but not overly impressed. "Ah."

Haley hesitated for a moment before glancing around. "I didn't know there was a zoo in Fox Springs."

Kate froze, caught off guard. "There's not!" she blurted out, her voice a little too quick. She fumbled for an explanation, trying to maintain her cool. "I'm, um, just traveling through... I'm seeing a horse... for the zoo. I'm only here for a bit."

Haley blinked, confusion briefly flashing across her face. But Kate's flustered charm was too attractive for her to care. Before the moment could grow awkward, the bartender returned, setting Kate's drink on the bar with a quick nod before leaving them to their conversation.

"I'm only in town for a few days, too," Haley said, smiling as she picked up her glass. "I guess this was lucky timing."

Kate nodded, feeling a wave of relief. "Definitely. What brings you to town?"

Haley's face clouded over for a second, her smile dimming. "Uh, dumb family stuff. I'd rather not talk about it."

Kate gave her an understanding smile, her own thoughts flashing to the ranch and everything she'd left behind for the night. "I understand dumb families."

Haley's expression lightened, and she raised her glass with a grin. "To dumb families!"

"To dumb families," Kate echoed, clinking her beer against Haley's glass.

They both took a drink, the clink of their glasses punctuating the growing tension between them, the chemistry undeniable.

Haley set her glass down, her eyes twinkling with mischief. "Cowgirl... what is your name?"

"Katherine," Kate replied, her voice soft but steady.

"Katherine," Haley repeated, her tone teasing, a playful glint in her eyes. "That's a pretty name for a pretty lady."

Kate shot her an unimpressed look, though the corner of her lips twitched with amusement.

Haley winced, immediately regretting the line. "That was a horrible line, wasn't it?"

"Yeah, it was," Kate said with a smirk, finally letting the playful tension ease into a smile. "But it was kinda cute, just like you are."

The atmosphere between them thickened, the attraction unmistakable as they exchanged lingering glances.

They clinked their glasses again, this time taking a really large drink, the alcohol easing the tension between them. Kate set her beer down with a smile, glancing sideways at Haley.

Haley grinned, clearly enjoying the banter. "Well, I'm staying at the lodge across the way."

Kate raised an eyebrow. "I am too."

Haley's grin widened. "What a happy coincidence. Should we... move this over there?"

Kate paused, her smile faltering slightly as she considered the offer. "I'm a little tipsy," she admitted, "and I might not be making great choices right now."

The honesty lingered between them, but the connection—the undeniable electricity—remained strong. Haley leaned in a little closer, her voice softer, more sincere.

"Well," Haley said gently, "I'm a little tipsy too, but we don't have to make any bad choices. Maybe we just... keep talking?"

Kate looked at her, weighing the moment. The night had unfolded so naturally—the easy conversation, the drinks, the shared smiles—and it had created a chemistry she hadn't anticipated. Slowly, Kate smiled, feeling herself relax.

"Yeah," she agreed, her voice warm. "I think I'd like that."

The next thing Haley knew, they were stumbling through her hotel door, their lips locked in a deep, urgent kiss. The soft click of the door closing barely registered as their bodies pressed together, their hands exploring each other in a desperate rush. Haley's back hit the wall, but she hardly noticed, too caught up in the heat of the moment. Kate's hands gripped her firmly, pulling her closer, their kisses growing more intense with every breath.

Their path toward the bed was far from graceful—bumping into chairs, nearly tripping over shoes—but none of that mattered. Every clumsy step felt electrified, their connection undeniable as they tore through the space between them and the bed. Kate's hands found the hem of Haley's shirt, and with one swift motion, she pulled it over Haley's head and tossed it to the side.

Haley gasped, her breath catching as Kate's lips found her neck, trailing kisses down her collarbone. She pulled Kate closer, her fingers tangling in Kate's hair, their bodies pressed together as they collapsed onto the bed. The sheets felt cool against her skin, but all Haley could focus on was Kate, her kisses, the warmth of her touch. She wanted Kate to touch every single inch of her body.

They were lost in the moment, completely wrapped up in each other, until Haley's phone pinged.

Haley froze, her lips pausing against Kate's skin, but she quickly pushed the sound out of her mind. Not now, she told herself, pulling Kate back to her, kissing her deeper. But then it happened again—her phone, then her laptop. The pings interrupted the moment, pulling Haley out of the haze.

Kate slowed, pulling back slightly, her brow furrowing. "You okay?" she asked softly.

Haley sighed, frustrated. "I'm so sorry... let me just..." She untangled herself from Kate, sitting up and reaching for her phone, the regret clear on her face.

Kate lay back, trying to play it cool but feeling the tension creeping in. She watched as Haley frantically checked her messages, the phone's light casting an unwelcome glow in the room.

"Oh, crap," Haley muttered, her eyes scanning the screen.

Kate raised an eyebrow, clearly annoyed but trying to keep her composure. "I'm guessing things aren't good?"

"No," Haley sighed again, her tone apologetic. "I am so sorry, it's an emergency. Our former social media director... went rogue. I had to fire him a couple of days ago. He's posting—"

Kate's frustration bubbled up. "Social media? That's the emergency?"

"In my line of work, it is," Haley said, glancing at her phone again.

Kate sat up, visibly annoyed now. "Interesting line of work," she said coolly, crossing her arms.

Haley winced, feeling the moment slip away. "I really wanted this... I wanted to be here with you... but—"

"But there's a social media emergency," Kate interrupted, standing up from the bed, her disappointment clear as she started to button her shirt.

"It's more than that," Haley explained quickly, scrambling to grab her own shirt from the floor. "We've got these big VC meetings coming up, and if they see a bad social media footprint, it could ruin everything."

She could tell Kate still looked confused, so she added, "VC stands for venture capital. These are the people who invest serious money to help companies like ours grow. They're incredibly picky, and they look at every little thing, especially online reputation. If they see anything negative, even just a bad post, they could decide we're too risky and pull out. And if that happens... everything we've worked for could go down the drain."

Kate wasn't buying it. She grabbed her jacket, her movements sharp and deliberate. "I'm not making this sound better, am I?" Haley asked, her voice tinged with guilt.

"No," Kate replied, her tone flat as she pulled her jacket on, clearly frustrated.

Kate glanced toward the door. "I hope you fix it." Then, with a sharp edge to her voice, she added, "If you didn't want to have sex with me, you could have just said so and not made up a social media emergency."

"Katherine, wait—" Haley reached out, but Kate was already walking away.

Without looking back, Kate opened the door and said, "Nice to meet you, Joan."

Haley stood frozen, watching as Kate walked out and quietly closed the door behind her. The air felt heavy, the room now eerily quiet.

With a defeated sigh, she grabbed her phone and laptop, crawling back onto the bed. She dialed quickly, her tone sharp with frustration. "Steve, how did Carl get into our social media accounts?"

The next morning, Haley lay in bed, utterly drained after spending half the night wrangling with the rogue social media emergency. Finally, the relentless pings and panic had subsided, leaving her in the peace and quiet she'd been longing for. She had barely drifted into a light sleep when a knock echoed through the stillness of her room.

Another knock.

Haley groaned, turning over in bed, her body protesting the interruption. "Seriously?" she muttered under her breath.

"Haley?" came a voice from the other side of the door.

Groggy and confused, Haley sat up, rubbing her eyes as she glanced toward the door. Reluctantly, she swung her legs over the edge of the bed and padded across the room, peeking through the peephole. A man stood on the other side, mid-to-late thirties, patiently waiting. He knocked again.

"Yes? Can I help you?" Haley called; her voice thick with sleep.

"I'm the Uber," the man replied, his tone matter of fact.

"The Uber?" Haley repeated, her confusion deepening.

The man cleared his throat, shifting slightly. "I'm Walter Wyman, Lucy's husband. Your brother sent me?"

Haley blinked, suddenly remembering the arrangement. She cracked the door open, the chain catching as she peered at him. "Oh, right! Sorry, I was up all night dealing with... an emergency."

Walter frowned slightly; his concern evident. "Oh, gosh. I'm sorry. Is everyone okay?"

Haley waved a hand dismissively. "Yeah, it was a social media emergency."

Walter's brow furrowed, looking genuinely puzzled. "That's a thing?"

"In my line of work..." Haley trailed off, shaking her head. "Never mind."

She glanced over Walter's shoulder and couldn't help but smirk when she saw the massive ranch truck idling behind him, a large Uber sticker plastered on the windshield. Only in Fox Springs, she thought with amusement.

"Give me a minute," she said, stepping back. "I need to pack up my stuff."

"Yeah, no problem," Walter replied. "I'll be in the truck."

As he turned to head back to the vehicle, Haley shut the door and hurriedly began gathering her things, stuffing her clothes into her suitcase and tossing her laptop into its case. Her mind raced as she packed, still replaying the events of the previous night. The disaster with Katherine, the social media debacle—it all swirled together, leaving her with a sense of unfinished business she couldn't shake.

Chapter 11

Haley stood on the front porch of the ranch, letting the stillness of the early hours wash over her. The porch, wrapped in festive Christmas decorations, looked as timeless as ever, its wide expanse offering a sweeping view of the fields she had once known so well. The crisp morning air carried the familiar scents of pine and fresh hay, filling her lungs with a sense of nostalgia she wasn't quite ready for.

She stared out at the fields, feeling a quiet ache. This land held so much of her past—so much of her heart. She had grown up here, running through those very fields with her parents' laughter echoing in the background. But that laughter had faded too soon. The emptiness of their absence still lingered, like a wound that had never fully healed.

Haley blinked against the memories, the bittersweet images of her parents replaced by the comforting faces of Meemaw and Pawpaw, who had raised her after the accident. She could still picture Pawpaw teaching her to ride a horse, his voice steady as he guided her reins, Meemaw watching with a proud smile. This place had been her refuge, their love the only thing that kept her grounded through the chaos of loss.

But that was a long time ago. It had been nearly a decade since she'd left, chasing a new life in the city. And yet, standing here now, the life she had built—successful as it was—felt far away, almost foreign.

This is where I came from, she thought, the weight of that realization settling in. This is what I left behind.

With a deep breath, Haley turned around and stepped forward, resting her hand on the worn doorknob of her childhood home. The ranch was more than just a place—it was a part of her, no matter how much time had passed. And now, after all these years, she was ready to step back inside and face whatever awaited her on the other side.

As soon as Haley stepped into the kitchen, the warmth of the familiar space washed over her. The kitchen was the heart of the home—just like it had always been. The large wooden table, worn from years of family meals, stood in the center, surrounded by sturdy chairs that had seen countless gatherings. The smell of freshly baked bread and something savory cooking on the stove filled the air. Copper pots hung from the ceiling, and lace curtains framed the window that looked out onto the fields, offering a perfect view of the land that held so many memories. The sunlight streamed in through the window, casting a soft glow across the room, making it feel both comforting and timeless.

Meemaw was bustling about as always, her red and green Christmas apron tied neatly around her waist, moving between the stove and the counter. The moment she spotted Haley, a big smile spread across her face, lighting up the room.

"Well, hey there, girl!" Meemaw exclaimed, pulling Haley into a tight hug. It was the kind of hug that made Haley feel instantly safe, loved, and at home.

"Look at you!" Meemaw continued, stepping back to admire her granddaughter. "Aren't you a sight for sore eyes."

"Hi, Meemaw," Haley replied, her smile soft and warm.

"My Christmas present," Meemaw said, her eyes twinkling with affection.

Haley's gaze shifted to Meemaw's ears, and she noticed the familiar glint of her grandmother's earrings. "Meemaw, you're wearing your fancy earrings... during the day?"

Meemaw reached up, her fingers lightly brushing the delicate earrings. "Oh, these old things? They were from your Pawpaw, remember?"

"I've always loved them," Haley said softly, her voice laced with affection for both her grandparents.

Just then, the front door swung open with a creak.

"Hey, Meemaw!" Charles called, stepping inside with his usual grin.

Meemaw turned toward the door, beaming with pride. "Haley's here!" she announced, her voice full of joy.

Charles walked over, wrapping Haley in a warm embrace. "Been a minute," he said, grinning as he stepped back.

Haley smiled, feeling a little more at ease with Charles there.

Meemaw, never one to sit still for long, bustled back toward the kitchen counter. "I'll get breakfast started," she said, already moving toward the stove, her hands as capable and comforting as always.

Haley watched her for a moment, a quiet sense of peace settling over her. Despite the lingering pain, there was still something healing about being home.

Charles stepped closer, setting his mug down and giving Haley a playful nudge. "So, big city girl, how's it feel to be back at the ol' ranch? Do you even know how to make coffee anymore, or do I have to re-teach you?"

Haley shot him a look, crossing her arms. "Please. I've been making coffee since I was ten. I'm just used to better coffee than this stuff you're drinking."

"Better coffee?" Charles repeated, pretending to be offended. "I see how it is. Too fancy for ranch coffee now, huh?"

"Maybe just a little," Haley teased, moving to grab a cup from the cabinet. She poured herself some coffee, taking a sip and wincing slightly at the bitterness. "Okay, yeah. You're right. This is terrible."

Charles laughed, leaning back against the counter. "Told ya! Guess city life's ruined you."

"Don't start," Haley warned playfully, raising an eyebrow at Charles.

Charles, still grinning, turned to her. "So glad you're here! Well, let's get you settled, and we'll have some breakfast."

"Sounds wonderful," Haley replied with a smile. But her tone shifted slightly as she asked, "How did the bank meeting go?"

Charles' smile faltered, the easy energy draining from his face. "Not great," he admitted quietly. "But we can talk about that later."

He started toward the stairs, but Haley hesitated, her gaze drifting toward the back door. She could almost feel the pull of the open fields beyond it, calling her back to the days when the ranch felt simpler.

"You coming up, sis?" Charles asked, pausing halfway up the steps, curiosity in his voice.

Haley turned back to him with a light laugh. "I just need to get settled and definitely take a scrub shower. The Fox Springs lodge is basically a part of me now." As soon as the words left her mouth, the memory of Katherine—her smooth skin, her scent—flooded her senses, sending a sudden flush of heat across her cheeks. She resisted the urge to touch her face, hoping Charles hadn't noticed.

Charles, oblivious, chuckled, well aware of the lodge's less-than-glamorous reputation. "Oh, well, you're staying here in the house.

"Um, no thank you," Haley replied quickly, shaking her head. "I'll stay in the cottage."

Charles raised an eyebrow. "I set up your old room."

Haley shook her head more firmly this time. "You know I don't like staying up there."

"All that therapy and you still can't sleep in your old room?"

"I can," Haley shot back, rolling her eyes. "I just love the cottage. It's cozy and peaceful. I'll stay there."

Charles crossed his arms, leaning against the banister with a smirk. "Kate lives there."

Haley's eyebrow shot up. "Oh, the perfect ranch hand, of course. She doesn't have her own place?"

"Nope," Charles said, shrugging. "She stays here. She's been a huge help."

Haley sighed, feeling her irritation rise slightly. "I know," she said, a little exasperated. "You've only mentioned how great she is in every conversation we've had the last three years."

Charles didn't miss a beat, shrugging again. "Well, you can see why it's helpful having her on the property. Come on, you'll survive."

Haley hesitated for a moment, but seeing Charles' persistence and knowing she didn't want to fight on her first day back, she gave in with an exaggerated sigh. "Ugh, fine," she muttered, relenting as she followed him up the stairs.

But the thought of superwoman ranch hand Kate lingered in the back of Haley's mind, tangled up with everything else this trip was stirring up. She wasn't ready to meet this woman—this stranger who had somehow managed to win over Meemaw and Charles like she could do no wrong. Haley couldn't quite put her finger on it, but Kate rubbed her the wrong way. Maybe it was because she was a little jealous—jealous that this woman had become so integrated into the family in her absence, taking a place that used to be hers.

"Let's go, dork," Charles teased, breaking her thoughts with a playful grin as he gestured for Haley to follow him up the stairs

As they made their way through the house, Haley trailed behind, her steps slower as the memories washed over her. Every creak of the floorboards, every familiar scent reminded her of a life she had been away from for too long. When they reached her old room, Charles stepped aside, letting her take it all in.

The room had barely changed. Haley chuckled softly as her eyes landed on the funny 90's posters still tacked to the walls—neon-colored pop bands and cheesy motivational quotes that had once felt so important to her younger self. A faded poster of Spice Girls was peeling in the corner, and beside it, "Hang in There" with a kitten dangling from a branch. It was a snapshot of a different time, one that felt light-years away from the life she lived now.

Her gaze drifted toward the dresser, where old family photos were arranged neatly on top. Her chest tightened as she stepped closer, her fingers tracing the edges of the frames. There were photos of her with Charles, the two of them grinning from ear to ear with Meemaw and Pawpaw, both of whom seemed to tower over them with protective warmth. One picture in particular showed her and Charles as kids, covered in dirt, standing next to Pawpaw after a long day in the fields. They were all laughing, the joy of that moment practically radiating from the photo.

But her eyes settled on another picture—one that made her pause. It was a snapshot of her with her parents, back when she was just a little girl. They were standing in front of the ranch on a sunny day, the fields stretching out behind them, the smiles on their faces so bright it was almost painful to look at. Haley picked it up, staring at her parents' faces for a long moment. The familiar ache stirred in her chest, the same one that always appeared when she thought of them. Their loss was always there, just beneath the surface.

She sighed softly, placing the photo back on the dresser, her hand lingering on the frame. The weight of their absence hung heavy in the air, mingling with the memories of Meemaw and Pawpaw, who had done everything they could to fill the void her parents had left behind.

As she glanced around the room once more—at the funny 90's posters, the family photos, the remnants of a simpler time—Haley felt a bittersweet mixture of love and loss.

As she closed her bedroom door, something familiar drifted up the stairs, cutting through the memories that weighed on her. The unmistakable smell of bacon filled the air, rich and savory, pulling her back to the present.

She paused at the top of the stairs, inhaling deeply, the scent stirring even more memories—but these were lighter, warmer. Breakfasts with Meemaw and Pawpaw, the kitchen always bustling with the sounds of sizzling bacon and the smell of fresh biscuits. It was one of the few constants on the ranch, no matter how much time had passed.

Haley made her way down the stairs, each step lighter now as the smell of breakfast grew stronger. By the time she reached the bottom, the kitchen was a comforting hum of activity, with Meemaw moving gracefully between the stove and the counter, her apron tied snugly around her waist.

Meemaw turned as they entered, a big smile spreading across her face. "Well, there you are!" she exclaimed. "I've got bacon and eggs almost ready. Sit yourselves down."

Haley felt the warmth of the kitchen settle over her like a soft blanket. The lingering sadness from upstairs began to ease, replaced by the comfort of being home—of being with family.

"Smells amazing," Haley said, her stomach growling in response.

"Sit down, girl," Meemaw said with a grin, motioning to the table. "Breakfast won't wait forever."

Haley smiled, taking a seat at the old wooden table, the same one that had seen countless family meals. For the first time in what felt like forever, she let herself relax, the smell of bacon and the comforting sounds of home making the weight of the past feel just a little bit lighter.

Meemaw stood at the kitchen island, the crackling sound of bacon sizzling in the pan filling the air, its rich, smoky smell drifting through the cozy space. The kitchen was just as Haley remembered—warm and inviting, with sunlight streaming in through the lace curtains that framed the window. The old wooden cabinets, slightly worn from years of use, added to the charm, and the familiar sight of copper pots hanging from the ceiling gave the room a sense of timelessness.

"How's your room?" Meemaw asked from the stove.

"It's good," Haley replied, feeling calm as she settled back into the rhythm of the ranch. The memories were still there, but for now, she allowed herself to focus on the present, the familiar comfort of Meemaw's kitchen easing the weight of the past.

Meemaw wiped her hands on her apron again, her tone light as she continued, "The Coopers' goats chewed through the fence again. Charles had to go wrangle 'em, bless his heart. He's been gone for a while now."

Haley grinned, shaking her head. "A goat?" she asked, amused. "Charles really isn't great at this, is he, Meemaw?"

Meemaw laughed, the sound warm and full of love. "He tries his best, but that boy sure does struggle with those animals sometimes. Even as a little one, he never really took to ranch life. He's got a good heart and a sharp mind for tech, but ranching? Well, let's just say he's more at home with computers than critters. But he loves the ranch and that means the world to me."

Haley picked up an apple from the basket in the middle of the table and took a bite, smiling at the thought of her brother chasing after rogue goats. In that moment, the ranch felt like home again, and for just a little while, the worries that had followed her melted away in the comfort of bacon, laughter, and Meemaw's kitchen.

Meemaw chuckled, shaking her head fondly. "You were always better at ranching than he was. Remember when you were ten and found that calf with her head stuck through the fence?"

Haley smiled, the memory brightening her face. "Yeah, I remember. Took me an hour to calm her down enough to get her head back through. She was scared out of her mind, but after some coaxing, we figured it out."

After a pause, Haley's smile faded slightly, and she looked at Meemaw, her voice growing more serious. "I really want to help, Meemaw," she said quietly, her fingers resting on the edge of the table. "With everything."

Meemaw's eyes softened as she reached across the table, her weathered hand resting gently on Haley's. The touch was comforting, grounding, as if all the strength Meemaw had carried over the years was transferred in that simple gesture. "I know you do, sweetie. I'm so glad you're here. Charles has been so stressed this past year. He doesn't think I notice, but I see it. It weighs on him, more than he lets on."

Before Haley could respond, the front door swung open with a loud creak, followed by the sound of boots shuffling across the wooden floor. Charles stumbled into the room, covered in dirt, his shirt streaked with sweat, and his hair disheveled like he'd been through a war. His chest heaved as he caught his breath, looking every bit like he had just lost a battle with a herd of wild animals.

"Well, here's the goat herder," Meemaw teased, a playful grin on her face as she took in the sight of him.

Charles wiped the sweat from his brow with the back of his hand, his face flushed. "They move a lot faster than you think," he muttered, out of breath but trying to regain some dignity as he plopped into the chair next to Haley.

Haley smirked, leaning forward. "Don't let it get your goat, or should I say... don't let the goat get your—"

"I got it, Hales," Charles interrupted with a tired laugh, waving her off as he reached for a piece of bacon. He took a bite, his exhaustion momentarily forgotten as he let out a satisfied groan. "Mmm... bacon."

Meemaw patted him on the arm affectionately as she moved back to the stove, watching him with a fond smile. "Come on, baby, eat up. Haley's ready to get to work on things around here."

Charles grabbed another piece of bacon from the plate and shoved it in his mouth, barely taking time to savor it before he stood up again, determination flickering back in his eyes. "No time like the present," he said, looking directly at Haley.

Chapter 12

Haley walked into the office, her heels tapping against the old wooden floor as she took in the cluttered space. The room was dimly lit, with stacks of paperwork strewn across the desk. The faint smell of coffee and dust hung in the air. Charles walked around her and sat behind the desk, leaning over a pile of papers, his brow furrowed in concentration.

"Here's where the revenue is coming from, where I've cut, and..." Charles began, shuffling through the paperwork and handing her a few sheets. His face looked tired suddenly, worn from months of worry.

Haley barely heard him as her eyes scanned the numbers on the page, her frown deepening. "The Christmas Hayride is down 60% from last year?" she interrupted, her voice sharp. "That's what's killing you. You were growing every year with the hayride and pumpkin patch, and this year... What's your marketing strategy?"

"Kate can talk more about that," Charles replied, his tone measured.

"Kate?" Haley raised an eyebrow, her frustration growing. "She's the reason you've lost revenue?"

"No," Charles said firmly, a hint of defensiveness creeping into his voice. "She's the reason it's grown in past years, but this year..."

Haley shook her head, the pressure mounting. "Well, this is the year that matters now. Looks like she's a drain on the ranch."

"That's not fair," Charles protested. "No, no—"

"You could start by cutting her out and renting the cottage as an Airbnb. She's a huge expense, and if the Christmas Hayride is..." Haley trailed off as her eyes caught movement near the doorway.

"...60% down," Kate's voice finished the sentence, cutting through the air as she stepped into the office. Haley spun around, her face flushing as she locked eyes with Kate.

"Hot Cowgirl," Haley muttered under her breath, the words slipping out before she could stop them.

Kate's eyes widened slightly in recognition. "The Berts opened their own Christmas Hayride to put us out of business, and it's working," she said, ignoring Haley's slip.

Charles, looking bewildered, cleared his throat. "Kate, this is Haley."

Kate's gaze sharpened as she turned to Haley. "Joan?"

"Haley," Charles corrected quickly. "Her name's Haley."

Kate's brow furrowed. "Wait—you're Haley? Haley is your name?"

Haley nodded, flustered. "Yes, it's Haley. Haley Joan Hollis."

"Right," Kate said, processing the revelation.

"And you're Katherine. You don't work at a zoo?" Hailey said.

Charles blinked, completely lost. "What? Zoo?"

Kate folded her arms, her expression unimpressed. "My friends call me Kate, and there are animals here. People look at them, so... kinda like a zoo. Should I call you Haley Joan? Or just Haley?"

"Just Haley," Haley shot back, her voice more defensive than she intended.

Charles looked between them, baffled. "Wait—do you two know each other?"

"No!" both women snapped in unison, glaring at each other.

Charles, still bewildered, threw up his hands. "Alright then..." He sighed. "Kate, your timing is perfect. Haley and I were just starting to go over the ranch business."

Kate glanced at Haley, sarcasm dancing in her eyes. "Dumb family stuff?"

Haley stiffened as Kate turned to address Charles. "I heard I'm an expensive line item," she said coolly, her tone edged with irritation.

"I didn't mean—" Haley started, but Kate cut her off.

"We've already had to cut people," Kate said, her frustration clear. "Running the hayride, moving the cows, dealing with animal emergencies, and managing upkeep with just two people is hard."

"I'm just looking at the numbers and the marketing—" Haley began, trying to regain control of the situation.

Kate shot her a cold glance. "Maybe we can solve this with some social media help. You know, since I'm so dumb about family stuff."

Charles looked from one woman to the other, utterly confused. "What in the world are you two talking about?"

Before Haley could respond, her phone rang. She glanced down, her face tightening as she recognized the name on the screen.

"I have to take this," Haley said abruptly. "It's my boss."

Without waiting for a response, she answered the call and walked out of the room, leaving Charles and Kate behind. Kate watched her go, her expression unreadable, before turning on her heel and leaving as well.

Charles stood in the office for a moment, staring at the door after Haley left, utterly baffled by the tension that had filled the room. He rubbed his temples, muttering, "What the hell just happened?" before letting out a long sigh.

Just as he gathered himself, he noticed Kate heading down the hall, her posture tense as she walked toward the kitchen. Without thinking, Charles followed her, the wooden floor creaking under his boots as he trailed behind.

When he reached the kitchen, Kate was already there, leaning against the counter, her arms crossed tightly over her chest. The kitchen was warm and inviting, the scent of freshly baked bread hanging in the air, but the atmosphere between them felt far from comfortable. Kate's jaw was clenched, and Charles could sense the frustration simmering just beneath the surface.

"Kate," he started gently, stepping further into the room. "What's going on with you and Haley?"

Kate shook her head, still not meeting his eyes. "Nothing," she muttered, her tone clipped.

Charles raised an eyebrow, clearly unconvinced. "Doesn't seem like nothing."

Kate grabbed a cookie from the table, taking a deliberate bite as Charles watched her with a raised eyebrow.

"What was all that about?" Charles asked in a different way, his voice laced with concern.

Kate chewed thoughtfully before replying, "All what about?"

"Haley didn't mean to suggest we fire you," Charles said, leaning against the table, trying to smooth over the tension.

"Yes, she did," Kate responded bluntly, not missing a beat.

Charles sighed, running a hand through his hair. "I really need her to love the ranch again, to see how much it means to us. Meemaw misses her."

Kate scoffed under her breath, shaking her head. "I'm not sure why."

Charles straightened up, his tone pleading. "Just be nice to her, please. It's only for a few days."

Kate rolled her eyes, but the comment Haley had made earlier about "dumb family stuff" still lingered, making her even more irritated. It wasn't just about Haley suggesting cutting her job—it was the way she'd brushed off the ranch, Meemaw, and everything Kate had come to see as her own family. The words stung, and that added to the growing dislike she felt toward Haley.

"Fine," Kate relented, though her voice was tight. "But I want her to stay out of my way. There's real work to do around here, and I don't have time to babysit someone who doesn't get it."

"Okay, okay," Charles agreed quickly, eager to avoid further conflict. "I'll make sure she stays out of your way, and please... try to be nice."

"I am nice," Kate said with a smirk, but the tension in her shoulders said otherwise as she turned and left the room.

***

Out on the porch, Haley stood with her phone pressed to her ear, pacing as she spoke with Eric. The peaceful view of the ranch stretched out before her, the rolling fields and distant hills bathed in golden sunlight. But Haley's mind was miles away, fixated on work.

"I want to give it one more look, Eric," she said, her tone sharp with focus.

"Great!" Eric replied, his voice buzzing with enthusiasm. "We've got solid interest, so let's push the numbers up by 20%. If this goes through, Hales, you could retire early—so kill it!"

Haley smiled faintly at the thought, but as she glanced out at the ranch, a flicker of something else stirred. Retire early? The idea was tempting, but there was a heaviness in her chest that wouldn't quite go away.

Haley paused for a moment, processing the news. "Okay, well, that's good news. I'll redo all the slides. I'll make those adjustments and get it to you tomorrow."

"It has to be tomorrow," Eric reminded her.

"It will be," Haley assured him, her voice firm but distracted.

As the call ended, she sighed, slipping her phone into her pocket. The peaceful view of the ranch stretched out before her, but her mind was still buzzing with work.

***

Meanwhile, out in the field, Charles and Kate worked side by side, moving the fence to open up a new pasture for the cows. Charles struggled with the task, his movements awkward and uncertain. But Kate moved with practiced ease, her hands skilled and steady, handling the job like she'd been doing it her whole life. Her natural proficiency made up for Charles' clumsiness, and together they managed the work.

The cows slowly ambled into the new pasture, and it became obvious that without Kate's help, the ranch would be a much more difficult place to manage. She was essential to the daily operations, her steady hand and quick thinking keeping everything running smoothly. Together, they shifted the fence line and moved the hen house, which sat on wheels, repositioning it as needed. The teamwork between them was evident, even if Charles relied on Kate more than he'd like to admit.

***

Inside the office, Haley sat at a desk piled high with paperwork, her brow furrowed as she studied the ranch's finances. Numbers spread across the sheets in front of her, and she frowned as they failed to add up the way she'd hoped. Sighing in frustration, she flipped through the papers again, lost in thought, until she sensed someone watching her.

Looking up, Haley spotted Meemaw standing in the doorway, a gentle smile on her face.

"Oh jeez! Meemaw, you scared me," Haley said, letting out a breath as she leaned back in the chair.

"I'm sorry, honey," Meemaw said softly, stepping into the room. "I love seeing you sit in that chair. How's it going?"

Haley rubbed her eyes, her frustration easing a little in Meemaw's presence. "Well, I'm trying to figure it all out. With the shift to intensive grazing, it's a lot more work than I realized."

Meemaw nodded thoughtfully. "Yep. Poor Charlie and Kate have to move the fencing every two days. With Adam gone, it's just the two of them now."

Haley flipped through more papers, her frown deepening. "And the Christmas Hayride revenue is down..."

Meemaw cut in with a sigh. "Because of the Berts!"

"The Berts?" Haley asked, raising an eyebrow.

"Yep," Meemaw replied, her tone sour. "They opened their own hayride in town, closer to people. Folks aren't wanting to drive all the way out here anymore."

Haley rolled her eyes in exasperation. "Ugh, Bert Jr. is a total creep." She picked up an envelope from the desk and slid out the paper inside. Her expression hardened as she read it. "And someone has made an offer to buy the place?"

"The Berts!" Meemaw spat, her voice dripping with disdain. "Those weasels think they can just take this place away. But I'm not sellin' to them."

Haley studied the offer, her expression conflicted. "Meemaw, I understand that, but... it's a solid offer. You could retire with this. Get a place in Fox Springs, stop working so hard."

Meemaw shook her head, her resolve firm. "That sounds horrible. I love working with Kate and Charles. I love this ranch. I'm not ready to walk away."

"I get that, but it's a lot of money," Haley said softly. "You wouldn't have to worry anymore."

Meemaw's expression softened, her voice quieter now. "I just wish I hadn't signed that loan..."

"You did what you had to do for Pawpaw," Haley said gently, trying to ease her grandmother's guilt.

Meemaw crossed the room and placed a hand on Haley's shoulder, her eyes full of emotion. "This place means everything to me, Haley. I want to give it to you and Charles. Not everything is about money."

"I know that," Haley replied, feeling a pang of guilt as she looked up at Meemaw. "Of course, it's not."

Meemaw's gaze drifted to the old photographs on the filing cabinet. She picked up one in particular—a picture of Pawpaw—and handed it to Haley.

"It's where your parents met. Where they got married. And where Pawpaw and I met too," Meemaw said, her voice filled with nostalgia. "I came one winter for the Christmas Hayride."

Haley had heard the story many times, but hearing it now, with the weight of the ranch's future on her shoulders, made it feel more poignant. She smiled as Meemaw continued.

"He was standing on a bale of hay, looking so handsome, and then the horse jerked," Meemaw recounted, her eyes distant as she remembered.

"And you fell into his arms," Haley finished, smiling softly.

Meemaw's grin widened. "And we kissed for the very first time."

Haley chuckled. "You always tell that part."

Meemaw's eyes sparkled as she looked at the photo in Haley's hands. "I think about him every day, Haley. This ranch... it's not just a business for us."

Haley's heart swelled at Meemaw's words. She nodded, feeling more determined than ever. "I'm not gonna give up. I'll keep trying to fix things."

Meemaw squeezed her shoulder. "That's my girl. If you want to make a real difference, talk to Kate. She knows this place better than anyone, and she loves it."

Haley shifted uncomfortably. "I don't think she likes me much."

"You'll win her over," Meemaw said with confidence. "The Christmas Hayride is about to start. Go out there and see what she's done."

"I haven't done the hayride in years," Haley admitted, a bit hesitant.

"Exactly!" Meemaw beamed. "It's about time. Kate's made it something special."

***

Out at the hayride area, the tractor was hooked up to a trailer lined with hay bales and strung with twinkling Christmas lights, casting a warm, festive glow over the field. Families gathered, sipping hot cocoa as they waited for the ride to begin. Kate stood on the trailer; her voice welcoming as she called out to the small group.

"Welcome to the Christmas Hayride! Grab yourself some cocoa, and we'll get started shortly!" Kate's smile was warm, though her eyes were focused on the task at hand.

As Kate scanned the crowd, her gaze landed on Haley walking toward the trailer.

"Hot cocoa's a nice touch," Haley said with a smirk as she approached, her breath visible in the cool night air.

"Oh, that's nothing," Kate replied, rolling her eyes. "Of course, Bert Jr. had to steal our ideas for their new hayride."

"We can agree they're snakes," Haley said, her tone light but knowing.

"Yes, they are," Kate agreed, shaking her head slightly. "You coming on the ride?"

"Yep," Haley nodded.

Kate gestured toward the trailer. "Need a hand getting up?"

Haley waved her off, determined. "I can handle a buckboard on my own."

Haley started to climb onto the trailer, her movements steady at first. But as soon as her foot touched the wooden slats, the trailer shifted beneath her, throwing her off balance. Before she knew it, Kate was there, her hands steadying Haley just in time. They froze for a moment, caught in an unintentional embrace, Haley's hand gripping Kate's arm for support while Kate's arms steadied her at the waist. For a brief moment, their eyes met. The closeness between them caught them both off guard, their breaths mingling in the crisp winter air. Time seemed to slow as they stood there, barely breathing, the warmth of their bodies cutting through the chill of the evening.

"The trailer shifted," Haley murmured, breaking the silence but making no effort to step away.

"They do that sometimes," Kate replied softly, her voice almost a whisper.

Haley cleared her throat, stepping back with a forced laugh. "I'll go get some cocoa."

Just like that, the moment passed. They turned away from each other, both regaining their composure as the cheerful buzz of the hayride filled the air again.

Kate moved through the crowd of eager passengers, handing out instruments—jingle bells, tambourines, and maracas. The group, already lively with excitement, began shaking the instruments, their voices soon blending into an offbeat but spirited version of Jingle Bells. Laughter echoed as the tractor slowly pulled the hay-filled trailer through the ranch, which was decorated with colorful, glowing Christmas lights. Reindeer, snowmen, and stars twinkled along the path, creating a magical atmosphere that made everyone forget the cold for a little while.

As the ride continued, Kate handed out reindeer antlers and bright red noses. One by one, the passengers donned the festive accessories, giggling as they saw each other transformed into a herd of reindeer. The biggest cheer of the night came when Kate, never one to shy away from fun, put on her own pair of antlers and nose. Even in the silly getup, there was something effortlessly charming about her.

With everyone now fully immersed in the Christmas spirit, Kate began telling the story of Rudolph the Red-Nosed Reindeer. As the hayride rolled through the ranch, they passed glowing tableaus, each one depicting a scene from the beloved tale. Large, light-up figures showed Rudolph, Santa, and the other reindeer. The first scene captured Rudolph standing sadly as the other reindeer laughed at his bright red nose.

"Here's poor Rudolph," Kate said, gesturing toward the tableau. "Made fun of for the very thing that made him special."

The group watched in silence, enchanted by the story. The tractor carried them slowly from one scene to the next, with Kate narrating each part of the tale with warmth and humor.

The next tableau showed Rudolph leaving the North Pole, his head hung low in sadness. Kate's voice took on a softer tone, drawing everyone into the heart of the story.

Finally, the trailer approached the last scene: Rudolph, proudly guiding Santa's sleigh through a blizzard, his bright red nose lighting the way. Soft, glowing lights bathed the tableau, and a snow machine puffed out additional flurries, mixing with the real snow already blanketing the ground. The extra layer of falling snow added to the magic, making the scene feel like a swirling winter wonderland, as if the moment had come to life straight from a holiday storybook.

"And here's Rudolph," Kate said, her voice brimming with pride, "saving Christmas with the very thing that made him different."

The group cheered, their excitement spilling over as the hayride came to an end. The trailer slowly rolled to a stop, but the festive energy remained high. Laughter bubbled over as the passengers clinked their cups of cocoa, and the final strains of Jingle Bells filled the air. Kate, always the showman, ended the song with a grand flourish, spreading her arms wide as the crowd burst into applause.

"Well, folks," Kate said with a warm smile, "that's the end of the hayride. Head on over to the fire pit, make some s'mores, and enjoy the rest of your evening. Merry Christmas!"

"Merry Christmas!" the group echoed as they disembarked, still smiling and laughing.

Haley lingered behind, standing next to Kate on the now-empty trailer. "That was so much fun," she said, her smile genuine. She glanced at Kate, taking in the antlers and red nose that still sat playfully atop her head. "The red nose suits you."

Kate raised an eyebrow, a smirk playing on her lips. "Yeah?"

"Yeah," Haley replied with a soft chuckle, meeting Kate's gaze. For a moment, the air between them seemed to crackle with something unspoken, something that neither of them were quite ready to name.

With a graceful hop, Kate jumped off the trailer and turned to help Haley down. Haley took her hand, landing lightly beside her.

"You've really outdone yourself," Haley said, glancing around at the twinkling lights and festive decorations. "This used to be just a few colored lights and some carols, but this... it's next level. The themes, the scenes—you've made it amazing."

Kate's face softened, clearly touched by the praise. "Thanks. It's been fun. Last year we did The Grinch."

"You really did a great job for the final year," Haley said, her tone shifting slightly.

Kate's smile faltered. "Final year?" she repeated, her eyebrows drawing together in confusion.

"Well, yeah... maybe," Haley said, her voice a little more cautious now. "I'm trying to stay positive for Meemaw and Charles, but..."

"So, you're just giving up?" Kate's voice sharpened, disbelief clear in her eyes.

Haley stiffened. "I'm the only practical one in this family. I need to make sure Meemaw can retire comfortably, and selling the ranch is the best way to make that happen."

"And what about Charles?" Kate asked, her tone growing colder.

"Charles will be fine," Haley said, brushing it off. "He worked in tech before this. He can find a job anywhere."

Kate shook her head, frustration creeping into her voice. "He loves this ranch." She paused, then added with a hint of sarcasm, "Maybe we should've done The Grinch again this year—would've suited you."

Before Haley could respond, Kate turned on her heel and started walking away. "I've got s'mores to help with."

Haley watched as Kate walked away toward the fire pit, her words still hanging in the air. After a moment, Haley sighed and turned, heading back toward the house, her thoughts heavy.

Chapter 13

Haley sat in the living room, her laptop casting a soft, bluish glow over her face in the otherwise dimly lit room. She typed the final line of her presentation and, with a small flourish, pressed the final key, the sense of satisfaction washing over her.

"And... voila!" she whispered to herself, a slight smile breaking through.

She quickly emailed the finished presentation to Eric, feeling the weight of the task lift off her shoulders. It was done—at least for now. With a long exhale, Haley leaned back in her chair, letting the tension slip away.

Her eyes drifted around the quiet room, taking in the warmth of the fire, the soft ticking of the wall clock, and the familiar creaks of the house settling around her. Her gaze fell on a family photo on the mantle, and she rose, drawn to it. She picked up the frame, holding it delicately, her fingers brushing over the image of herself as a young girl, sandwiched between her parents on a sunny day at the ranch.

The room felt heavier, somehow, the silence thickening. The familiar ache of their absence surfaced, raw and real, as if no time had passed since they'd been here. She remembered her father's easy laugh, her mother's gentle touch. The memories tugged at her, the empty space where they should have been—the part of her life they'd missed, the one she'd lived without them.

Tears welled in her eyes, and this time, she couldn't hold them back. The quiet sobs escaped, breaking the silence. She clutched the photo tighter, the grief spilling out in waves, mingling with years of unspoken pain, the sorrow of all the milestones, big and small, that they'd already missed as well as the ones they'd never see.

As her shoulders shook, she felt a soft, comforting hand on her shoulder. Startled, she looked up to see Meemaw standing beside her, her eyes filled with understanding.

"Oh, honey," Meemaw whispered, gently pulling her into a hug. "It's alright. I miss them, too."

Haley sank into Meemaw's embrace, allowing the warmth to seep in. They stood in silence, holding each other as the shared weight of loss brought them even closer. Meemaw's hand stroked her hair soothingly, her quiet presence grounding Haley.

After a while, Meemaw pulled back slightly, meeting Haley's gaze. "They'd be so proud of you, you know? Of everything you've done and the woman you've become."

Haley managed a small, watery smile. "I hope so," she whispered, her voice thick with emotion. "Sometimes it feels like... I don't know, like I'm doing all this just to keep moving, just to keep from feeling how much I miss them."

Meemaw nodded, a soft sadness in her eyes. "It's hard, Haley. Losing people we love changes us. But you've still got a family here, and we're all proud of you."

They sat down together at the table, the comforting smell of coffee lingering in the air from earlier. Meemaw took Haley's hand in hers, her grip strong but gentle.

"You know," Meemaw began, "I still talk to your Pawpaw every day. Ask him what he'd do about things here. I feel him with me, guiding me. And maybe, in some way, they're still with you too."

Haley looked down at their intertwined hands, nodding. "I think I'd like to believe that."

Meemaw squeezed her hand, a quiet smile spreading across her face. "You don't have to do it all alone, you know. You've got Charles and me, and even Kate, despite how prickly she can be."

Haley chuckled softly, wiping her eyes. "Yeah, she's got a bit of a... tough exterior."

Meemaw laughed. "That's one way to put it! But she loves this place, just like you do. I know the two of you will find some common ground."

Haley sighed, a hint of weariness creeping back in. "I'm trying, Meemaw. It's just... it's hard being here again, knowing everything that's at stake and all these memories coming up."

Meemaw gave Haley's hand another gentle squeeze, her eyes soft with wisdom and understanding. "You know, honey, sometimes I write Pawpaw letters. Just little notes, really, about my day, or if I'm feeling low or missing him. I tuck them away in a little box by my bed. It's not much, but it makes me feel close to him, like he's still here, listening."

Haley looked up, curiosity flickering in her eyes. "Letters?"

"Yes," Meemaw nodded, her gaze distant for a moment as though she were seeing those letters in her mind. "It's a way to talk to him, even though he's not here in the flesh.

Just little things—moments I want to share or things I think he'd laugh at. It keeps his spirit close."

Haley considered it, a small, thoughtful smile tugging at her lips. "Maybe I'll try that. There's so much I wish I could tell them... about everything."

Meemaw's eyes brightened. "You should. Write it all down. It can be a comfort in ways you might not expect. And who knows—maybe they're reading every word."

They sat in comfortable silence, the weight of the moment shifting, softened by their shared understanding. After a moment, Meemaw stood and gently kissed Haley on the forehead. "Get some rest, honey. Tomorrow's a new day."

Haley watched her go, feeling the ache in her chest ease a little, the room's quiet now more of a comfort than a burden. She took one last glance at the family photo before setting it back on the mantle. With a deep breath, she shut her laptop, turned off the light, and headed up to bed, carrying with her the warmth of her family's love.

***

The soft light of morning filtered into the small office, casting a warm glow on the weathered desk where Haley sat, a steaming cup of coffee in hand as she sifted through financial reports. Her eyes were focused, brows knitted as she scanned the numbers, occasionally pausing to take a long sip.

Her concentration was interrupted by a light knock on the doorframe. Charles leaned in, his face relaxed but a bit cautious. "Hey, breakfast is ready," he said, a hint of amusement in his voice.

Haley barely looked up, her eyes still on the papers. "Thanks, but I'm good," she replied. "Coffee's all I usually have."

Charles smirked, stepping into the room and leaning casually against the doorframe. "You got that big presentation off your plate?"

"Yes, thank goodness," Haley sighed, setting her cup down with relief. "And I went on the hayride last night."

"Oh, yeah?" His eyes lit up. "Kate went with the Rudolph theme this year."

"She did a great job," Haley admitted, a smile softening her features. "It was fun. Too bad about the Berts undercutting the whole event, though."

"Tell me about it," Charles muttered, his expression darkening. He moved to sit across from her, rubbing the back of his neck. "We've lost so much revenue to them... There has to be another way to make it up."

Haley looked up, meeting his eyes with a gentle smile. "Well, I've gone over the books, and you keep everything impressively organized."

Charles grinned, feigning a smug expression. "Not just a pretty face, you know."

Haley chuckled, then her tone turned serious. "But honestly, this loan... It's a big weight. If the hayride wasn't down so much, it'd be manageable. But as it stands..."

Charles sighed, leaning back in his chair and staring at the ceiling. "Meemaw and I hoped you'd see something we hadn't. Some brilliant idea or loophole."

"I wish I could just wave a magic wand and make it work," Haley said, shaking her head. "Outside of a miracle refinance, though…"

"Yeah. No luck there," he replied, frustration evident in his voice.

Suddenly, Haley's phone buzzed on the desk, lighting up with Eric's name. She glanced at Charles with an apologetic smile. "I've got to take this. He's probably requesting some last-minute changes."

Charles nodded, standing up. "No worries. I'll go grab some bacon before Meemaw eats it all. Sure you don't want anything?"

"I'm good," she replied, giving him a grateful smile before answering the call. "Hey, Eric. Yep, I can make those changes."

Charles left quietly as Haley opened her laptop, her fingers returning to the keyboard as she focused back on her work, her mind slipping back into the world she'd almost escaped for a few precious hours.

***

Haley finished the presentation, hoping this would finally be the last edit it needed. She closed her laptop just as Meemaw appeared in the doorway.

"This right here is hot cocoa made from Pawpaw's world-famous recipe," Meemaw said with a warm smile, holding out a thermos. "It's Kate's favorite. Head down to the cottage and extend an olive branch."

Haley sighed, leaning back in her chair. "She hates me."

Meemaw gave her a knowing look. "She doesn't know you."

Haley hesitated, her voice quieter. "Are you worried about losing the ranch?"

Meemaw didn't miss a beat. "No."

"Why not?" Haley asked, confused by her calm confidence.

Meemaw's eyes sparkled with the certainty of years of wisdom. "Because I know I'm gonna be on this ranch for a long time, just like I know the sun will rise and the wind will blow. There's a feeling in my bones that tells me to trust—trust in you, Charles, and Kate."

Haley looked down, doubt creeping into her expression. "What if I don't figure it out?"

Meemaw reached out, resting a comforting hand on Haley's arm. "Well, something will happen. I know it, honey. Haven't you ever just known something—something that doesn't make sense, but you just know it's true?"

Haley chuckled softly, shaking her head. "Only in romantic comedies."

Meemaw smiled, her eyes twinkling with amusement. "Well, my life's been one real romantic comedy, then. You don't have to worry like this, Haley girl. We just have to do what we can, one step at a time. It's gonna work out. So no, I'm not really worried."

Haley's expression softened as she met Meemaw's steady gaze. "I hope I have that kind of trust one day."

Meemaw winked. "You will. Now, take this to Kate for me, please."

"Alright," Haley said with a small smile. "Just for you."

"Thank you," Meemaw said, patting her cheek.

Haley took the thermos and kissed Meemaw on the cheek before heading out.

Stepping outside, thermos in hand, she realized she'd forgotten her jacket. She shivered as the wind picked up, the snow already falling heavily. Pulling her arms tight around herself, she made her way toward Kate's cottage through the swirling snow.

She glanced back at the warm light spilling from the house, briefly considering going back for her jacket but deciding against it. She clutched the thermos to her chest to keep herself warm.

The ranch was quiet, the usual daytime sounds softened under the weight of night and snow. Her breath formed small clouds as she exhaled, her steps cautious on the slick ground. Despite the cold, something about the walk felt peaceful, like the ranch itself was taking a deep breath under the winter sky.

Haley approached the small, cozy cottage nestled among the trees at the edge of the property. Warm light glowed through the windows, illuminating a cute Christmas wreath on the door. She took a steadying breath, rubbing her arms briskly against the chill. As she knocked lightly on the door, she silently cursed herself for thinking she could brave the snow without a jacket.

Inside the warm cottage, Kate was stirring a pot of deer stew on the stove, filling the air with the rich, savory aroma of simmering vegetables and spices, when a knock sounded at the door. Her brow furrowed in confusion—no one would come all the way out here in this weather. She glanced out the window, noting the thick blanket of snow covering the ground, and the swirling flurries obscuring the view.

Setting down the ladle, she moved to the door and pulled it open, only to find Haley standing there, completely disheveled, her hair plastered with snow and a shiver running through her body. She didn't have a jacket, and the wind whipped her hair across her face, sending a shower of snowflakes into the room.

"I come in peace," Haley said, her voice wry but visibly shivering as her breath formed puffs in the frigid air. "Brought hot cocoa," she added, holding up a thermos.

Kate's eyes widened as she quickly reached out, grabbing Haley's arm and pulling her inside, slamming the door against the biting cold. "Are you nuts?" she exclaimed, looking her up and down with disbelief. "It's freezing out there. That is a full-blown snowstorm, by the way, and you're dressed like... like you're on a coffee run in the city."

"Yeah," Haley muttered, teeth chattering as she tried to play it off with a smile. "In retrospect, maybe not my best idea."

Kate shook her head in exasperation. "Here, sit by the fire. You look half-frozen." She guided Haley over to the roaring flames, then grabbed a blanket from a nearby chair and wrapped it around her. "You'll have to warm up first before that cocoa can even help."

Haley shot her a small smile, holding the thermos."Meemaw mentioned it's your favorite," she murmured, snuggling deeper into the blanket as the warmth of the fire began to seep into her bones.

Kate smirked, rolling her eyes affectionately. "City girls," she muttered, but the playful tone in her voice softened her words. The two of them stood there, letting the cozy warmth settle around them, a comfortable quiet lingering in the small room.

"Stay by the fire," Kate instructed. "I'll grab some cups."

Haley moved closer to the flames, letting their warmth begin to chase away the cold that clung to her. She closed her eyes, taking in the comforting smell of stew that filled the room. Moments later, Kate returned with two steaming mugs.

"Smells amazing," Haley said, opening her eyes. "What is that?"

"Deer stew," Kate replied, her smile softening. "Pawpaw's recipe."

Haley's face tightened, a hint of annoyance creeping into her voice. "Meemaw gave you his recipe?"

Kate raised an eyebrow, a playful glint in her eyes as she handed Haley the mug of cocoa. "She did. And maybe, I'll let you have some... if you're nice to me."

Haley smirked, taking a slow sip from her mug. "I trudged through a snowstorm to bring you hot chocolate. Does that count as nice?"

"I suppose so. It is my favorite hot chocolate." Kate said with a teasing smile.

They lingered in comfortable silence for a moment, letting the warmth of the fire and the sweetness of cocoa settle between them.

Kate broke the quiet, raising an eyebrow. "So, you really came out in this weather just to bring me cocoa?"

Haley shrugged, glancing down at her mug. "Well, it was Meemaw's idea," she admitted. "She thought you might have some insight on how to save this place."

Kate's expression softened, though there was a touch of doubt in her eyes. "That's hopeful of her. I'd love to be that kind of help, but... I don't know if I can. I've looked at those numbers myself, and honestly? That bank loan feels like highway robbery."

Haley nodded, her voice dropping. "Yeah. I know."

Kate let out a resigned sigh, leaning back against the counter as she processed the weight of it. "I can't see any way around it. I mean, I didn't go to Harvard or anything..."

"Dartmouth," Haley corrected, her tone light but somehow reassuring.

Kate's lips curved into a small smile. "Dartmouth," she repeated, as if tasting the word.

"You don't need an Ivy League education to see how much trouble this place is in," Haley replied, her tone edged with frustration. "You just need a calculator."

Kate's brow furrowed, her eyes searching Haley's. "But you haven't told them yet, have you?"

Haley let out a sigh, the weight of it evident. "I have," she admitted. "But Meemaw keeps hoping I'll have some brilliant idea to fix it all."

Kate's gaze softened. "That's a lot to carry, Haley."

Haley nodded, her shoulders slumping slightly. "And I've got nothing. No miraculous plan, no last-minute save. Just... nothing."

They stood there in silence for a beat before Kate spoke, her voice thoughtful. "Maybe if you got to know the ranch again, really know it, that idea might come. Sometimes inspiration sneaks up on you, you know?"

Haley raised an eyebrow. "I already went on the hayride."

Kate chuckled, shaking her head. "There's more to the ranch than just the Christmas hayride, you know," she said gently. "Spend a little time here—get reacquainted with the place. You never know what might spark an idea, and, honestly, it could be good for you to just breathe out here. Maybe even enjoy it."

Haley shrugged, a hint of defensiveness in her voice. "I like the city."

Kate smirked, a hint of amusement in her eyes. "You know I'm right."

Just then, the lights flickered once, twice, and then went out completely, plunging the room into sudden darkness.

"Um... what is happening?" Haley asked, her voice tinged with alarm as her eyes darted around the now pitch-black room.

"Power's out," Kate replied casually, already moving toward the fireplace with practiced ease.

"I can see that. But why?" Haley's voice was high, her body tense as she stood frozen in place.

"Snowstorm," Kate said with a shrug, kneeling to stoke the fire as if this was the most normal thing in the world.

Haley blinked, still processing. "Don't you have a generator?"

Kate chuckled softly, glancing over her shoulder. "Nope. But I have a fireplace, plenty of water, and enough supplies. We'll be just fine."

As Kate spoke, Haley grabbed her phone, frantically unlocking it, only to stare in horror at the screen. "I have no service!" she exclaimed, her eyes wide with a mixture of panic and disbelief.

Kate continued stoking the fire, clearly unfazed. "Yeah, the tower's probably down. Happens a lot in storms like this. Power goes, then cell service. It's normal."

Haley's breathing quickened, and she began pacing back and forth, her hands gripping her phone tightly. "So, we're just stranded here? No heat, no power, no Wi-Fi?"

Kate smiled to herself as she finished building the fire. "We've got heat, Haley. It's called a fire. And this place is cozy enough that it'll stay warm as long as we keep it going. No need to panic."

Haley stopped pacing, watching Kate with disbelief. "You're seriously calm about this."

Kate shrugged, brushing off her hands as she stood up. "You city girls really don't know how to live without a signal, do you?"

"This is not funny," Haley shot back, glancing at the fire as she tried to calm her own nerves. "I'm not exactly used to roughing it." "Oh my God," Haley groaned, running a hand through her hair. "My email. I don't have access to my email! Thank God I sent the presentation, but Charles has no idea where I am."

"We'll call over there," Kate said, walking over to a small table in the corner.

"Call?" Haley asked incredulously. "How are we supposed to call? I have no service! I'm completely cut off!"

With a slight smile, Kate picked up the handset of an old CB radio and pressed the button. "Ranch Babe to Big Mama."

Haley blinked, her disbelief giving way to bemusement. "Ranch Babe?"

A crackly voice came through the radio, warm and steady. "This is Big Mama. Go ahead, Ranch Babe."

"Just letting y'all know the power is out, but we're safe and sound," Kate said into the radio, her tone relaxed.

"Alright, good to hear," Meemaw's voice crackled in response. "Y'all got everything you need?"

"That's a 10-4, Big Mama. We're gonna wait out the storm," Kate replied with a grin.

"10-4, Ranch Babe. Holler if you need anything. Over and out."

Haley stared at the radio, her jaw slightly dropped. "Wow."

Kate shrugged, a playful grin spreading across her face. "Hey, I didn't pick my handle."

"Sure, you didn't," Haley said, still processing the whole exchange.

Kate smirked, standing up. "I'll grab some candles."

As Kate rummaged in a nearby cabinet, Haley dipped a spoon into the pot of stew and took a tentative bite. Her eyes closed in delight as the rich, savory flavor hit her. "Ooohhh, that is good."

As Kate returned with her arms full of candles, she caught sight of Haley's contented expression as she savored another bite of stew. Moving around the room, Kate carefully placed the candles, their flickering flames casting a warm, romantic glow over the space. "What's that look for?" she asked, curiosity tinged with affection.

"Hmmm," Haley murmured, her voice carrying a hint of nostalgia. "Just like I remember."

Kate's smile softened as she glanced at her. "Good. Are you still cold?"

"A little," Haley admitted quietly.

Without hesitation, Kate grabbed a thick, warm blanket from the nearby chair and draped it over Haley's shoulders, tucking it gently around her. "Here," she said softly. "This should help." She gave Haley's shoulder a reassuring squeeze before settling back, watching as Haley pulled the blanket tighter, the warmth beginning to ease the chill.

"Thank you," Haley said.

After a few moments, Haley began to fidget, clearly not used to the silence stretching on for so long. She glanced around the small room, her eyes landing on an old paperback sitting on the coffee table. Curious, she reached over, picked it up, and squinted at the worn cover.

"The Tuscany Madonna?" she read aloud, a smirk playing on her lips as she held up the novel, eyeing Kate with amusement.

Kate turned around, her eyebrows raising slightly. "Don't judge too hard. That's Meemaw's stash of guilty pleasures. The woman has a soft spot for sappy romances."

Haley chuckled, flipping the book over in her hands. "Didn't peg her for the type."

"Oh, she'd be horrified if she knew I let that secret slip," Kate said with a laugh, settling herself in a nearby chair. "But trust me, you'll find a stack of these hidden somewhere in just about every room here."

Haley thumbed through the yellowed pages, the scent of old paper mingling with the smell of stew and firewood. "So, you're saying there's no chance you've ever read this... maybe even secretly enjoyed it?"

Kate shrugged, feigning indifference. "Maybe once or twice. Just for research purposes, of course."

Haley grinned, putting the book down. "Research, huh? Something tells me you're not exactly immune to the charms of Tuscany, lost lovers, and dramatic reunions."

Kate rolled her eyes playfully, folding her arms. "And here I thought city girls were the practical types."

"Oh, we are," Haley replied, settling deeper into her chair. "But everyone likes a little romance now and then."

They fell into a comfortable silence, the flickering fire casting soft shadows that danced around the room.

Haley thumbed through the book for a minute, quickly losing interest and setting it back down. As the silence stretched on, she started fidgeting, her patience wearing thin. Finally, she broke the quiet.

"So, Ranch Babe..." she teased, glancing over with a mischievous smile.

Kate rolled her eyes, amused but clearly not ready to take the bait. "You really can't just sit in silence, can you?"

"I can too," Haley replied, feigning offense. "I'm always the quietest one in my group meditation."

Kate gave her a dry look. "Oh, I'm sure."

Ignoring the sarcasm, Haley shifted in her seat, refusing to let the conversation stall again. "Fine, let's try this 'getting to know you' thing again. No sarcasm this time."

Kate sighed, finally giving in. "Alright, what do you want to know, Joan?"

Haley shot her a playful glare, deciding to let the jab slide. "Where are you from? What brought you out here? What makes you... well, you?"

"Oh, so you want to hear about my awkward, dysfunctional family history?" Kate asked, raising an eyebrow.

Haley gave her a pointed look. "Well, you know mine pretty well by now."

Kate sighed, leaning back and crossing her arms. "Alright, fine. Originally, I'm from Kentucky—Lexington. My parents were in the horse business. They bred and trained horses, some of them top-tier, like Triple Crown contenders."

"Seriously? There must've been a lot of money in that," Haley replied, surprised.

"Oh, sure," Kate said, her tone dry. "And a lot of rich kids parading around on horses they didn't know the first thing about caring for."

Haley's eyebrows shot up. "Wait, like the whole getup? Little helmets, riding pants, whips, and all that?"

Kate laughed, nodding. "Yep. The whole deal. Private school, pageants, lavish 'charity' galas. The full Southern debutante experience."

Haley smirked, trying to picture it. "Kate, the rich princess. That really doesn't seem like you at all."

Kate rolled her eyes, but her lips turned into a smile. "Trust me, it wasn't. I gave it my best shot, though. But I didn't exactly fit the pageant queen mold they had in mind. I tried to play the part, at least for a while. I did everything they expected—perfect daughter, obedient, all that."

Haley leaned in, intrigued. "So, what changed?"

"I loved working with the horses; that part felt real," Kate began, her expression turning serious. "But the people—the fake smiles, the pretentious 'friends'—I was never going to be happy living that way. My parents had this dream of me as some junior league beauty queen, but all I wanted was to be a cowgirl and, well... maybe date the other 'princesses' instead."

"Ah," Haley replied, her voice softening with understanding.

"Yeah," Kate continued, her voice low. "Their money, their rules. I couldn't keep pretending, so I left."

"Wow," Haley said, leaning forward, captivated. "Where did you go?"

"Texas, New Mexico... places where I could just be me, no family name, no expectations," Kate replied. "Eventually, I ended up here. It felt like a real chance to start fresh. Your grandparents and Charles never cared about all that background stuff. You're lucky to have them."

Haley nodded, her voice soft. "I know I am." She hesitated, then asked, "So you haven't spoken to your family at all since then?"

Kate shook her head. "No. We had a pretty big blowout before I left. We're all too stubborn to pick up the phone."

"Too stubborn? You?" Haley teased, a gentle smile tugging at her lips.

Kate managed a small grin. "Yep. Me."

"I'm sorry," Haley said, her tone sincere. "That's... a lot to carry."

"Yeah." Kate's smile faded, and for a moment, a heavy silence settled between them.

The fire crackled softly as Kate stood and made her way over to the pot of stew, the warm light casting shadows across her face as she ladled more into their bowls. Haley watched her, sensing a vulnerability beneath Kate's calm demeanor, and felt a quiet understanding pass between them, bridging their worlds just a little bit more.

When Kate returned, she settled onto the couch beside Haley, silently sipping her stew. After a moment, she broke the quiet. "So, what about you? What's your story?"

Haley smirked, arching a brow. "Seriously? You, Charles, and Meemaw don't talk about me all the time?"

Kate chuckled, nodding. "Lately? Yeah, we do. You're like the last-minute angel who swoops in to save the day."

Haley sighed, running a hand through her hair. "Usually, I thrive in high-pressure situations. But this... this is different. I have no idea why they think I've got some brilliant solution up my sleeve."

"Maybe it's because you grew up here," Kate suggested, a note of encouragement in her voice.

Haley let out a small laugh. "Yeah, but a lot of that time was spent as a moody teenager," she admitted.

"Really?" Kate raised an eyebrow, surprised. "I've seen some photos of you riding with your parents," she added gently. "You looked like you might've even been enjoying it."

"I did ride," Haley replied quietly, her voice tinged with a mix of nostalgia and something heavier. "But I don't really talk about it."

Kate softened, recognizing the hesitation in her tone. She chose not to press further, knowing it likely touched on the loss of Haley's parents—something Meemaw and Charles had mentioned over the years. Instead, she followed Haley's gaze to the fire.

"The fire's dying down," Haley said, her voice steady but distant. "How do you keep it going while we sleep?"

Kate shrugged, understanding her need to shift topics. "I don't. First ranch lesson: fires go out when they aren't tended to."

Haley gave a faint smile, her gaze flicking to the small twin bed in the corner. "That's true for a lot of things," she murmured, her voice soft.

Kate followed Haley's line of sight and gave a small sigh. "So, umm... you can't go back out in this storm. Not tonight."

Haley raised an eyebrow, a smirk playing on her lips. "Oh? And how's that going to work?"

Kate gestured to the small twin bed in the corner. "You can take the bed, of course."

"And you'll be where, exactly? Sleeping here on this sofa? I'm pretty sure it's more decorative than functional."

Kate shrugged, trying to play it off. "It's fine. I've crashed here plenty of times."

Haley crossed her arms, tilting her head. "Kate, let's be honest—it's tiny, and you're way too tall for it. You'd actually fit better in the bed—with me."

Kate's expression remained stubborn, her arms crossing, "Not happening."

Haley leaned forward, a glint of mischief in her eyes. "Come on, it'd be warmer. Purely practical, Ranch Babe."

"Ranch Babe?" Kate raised an eyebrow, fighting back a smile.

Haley shrugged with a sly grin. "Well, it suits you. And let's be real, it's not like we have many options."

"I'll be fine on the sofa," Kate insisted as she stood up. "I sleep outside in this weather all the time."

"Right. Ranch Babe. Tough as nails. Impervious to discomfort. Got it," Haley said, rolling her eyes.

Kate chuckled, reaching into a dresser and pulling out a set of flannel pajamas and thick socks. She tossed them to Haley. "Here, these should keep you warm."

Haley caught them with a grin. "A pair of thermal pajamas, huh? Now we're talking."

She headed to the bathroom to change, while Kate quickly changed into her own flannels. A few minutes later, Haley strolled out, trying to look casual as she crossed the room and slipped under the covers.

"Good luck with that couch," Haley said, a hint of mischief in her half-smile.

"The ranch is going to be a mess after this storm," Kate murmured. "I'll need to get up early."

"Right," Haley replied quietly, settling into the bed. "Well, goodnight, Ranch Babe."

Kate smiled in the dark. "Goodnight, city girl."

***

Kate lay across the narrow couch, bundled under what felt like a mountain of blankets. She blew out the last candle beside her, casting the room into near darkness, with only the faint glow of the fire illuminating the space. Haley, still wide awake in the bed, listened as Kate tossed and turned, each rustling shift revealing her discomfort. Despite all the blankets, the chill in the room was undeniable, and both women were clearly shivering.

"How's it going over there?" Haley called softly, trying not to sound too amused.

"Fine," Kate replied, her teeth chattering slightly. "Super comfortable."

"Yeah?" Haley teased, raising an eyebrow she knew Kate couldn't see. "You sure are moving around a lot for someone who's comfortable."

"Just trying to get... situated," Kate mumbled, shifting yet again.

Haley smirked, though her voice softened. "Kate, I can hear your teeth chattering from here."

"I'm fine," Kate insisted, but her shivering betrayed her words.

Haley sighed, sitting up slightly. "Look, I'm not going to sleep if you're tossing and turning all night. This is silly. Just come over here."

"I told you, I'm okay," Kate protested, though her resolve was starting to sound weaker.

"Well, I feel bad for taking your bed," Haley countered. "So, if you won't move for yourself, then do it for me, alright?"

There was a pause as Kate considered, finally realizing how ridiculous she must look wrapped up like a burrito and still freezing. She exhaled, the cold biting more than her pride.

"Now I feel bad that you feel bad," Kate admitted quietly.

"Good. Come on, then," Haley said, patting the space beside her.

"Fine," Kate relented with a sigh.

She climbed off the couch, crossing over to the bed with a slight hesitation, eyeing the narrow space. Standing by the bed, she pondered how they'd both fit without it getting... complicated. The bed was definitely small, and the only way they'd both fit was if they didn't try to avoid each other.

"Um, maybe back-to-back?" Kate suggested, a bit unsure.

Haley gave her a playful smirk. "Not enough room for that. Looks like we're going to have to—well, you know."

"Spoon," Kate finished for her.

"Yes. Survival spoon," Haley replied with mock seriousness.

"Right," Kate nodded, playing along.

"Exactly. Survival," Haley continued, smirking. "And since I'm the fragile city girl here, I should obviously be the small spoon."

Kate couldn't help but laugh softly. "Obviously."

"Alright, here we go," Haley said, bracing herself as she adjusted to make room.

Kate climbed into the narrow bed, the warm glow of the fire casting soft, flickering shadows over them. She carefully squeezed in behind Haley, both of them hyper-aware of the limited space. It was undeniably awkward, and Kate tried to keep her movements gentle, though they still bumped a few times in the process.

"Your arm is digging into my back," Haley muttered, trying to adjust.

"Sorry," Kate whispered, shifting to ease the discomfort. "Told you it'd be a little tight."

"Maybe if you just..." Haley reached for Kate's arm, pulling it around her waist, allowing Kate to settle more naturally. The closeness was unexpectedly calming, and they both relaxed a little.

"Okay, that's better?" Kate asked softly, adjusting herself so they fit as comfortably as possible.

"Yeah, I think that's the only way this works. Spatial efficiency, you know?" Haley replied, her voice gentler now.

"Right. Physics," Kate said, smiling against the back of Haley's shoulder.

"Yes. Definitely physics," Haley murmured, her voice quieter as the warmth of the fire and Kate's presence began to lull her.

For a moment, they lay there in silence, both feeling the strange but undeniable comfort of sharing the small bed. The warmth slowly seeped in, relaxing their bodies, and Haley let out a contented sigh.

"It is toasty, wow," Haley remarked, the warmth finally starting to sink in.

"It's kind of nice, right?" Kate asked, her voice soft.

"It is," Haley admitted.

"I mean, it's warm. And we won't freeze. So that's nice," Kate added.

"That is nice," Haley agreed, her voice fading as sleep started to take over.

"Goodnight, Kate," Haley murmured.

"Night, Haley," Kate replied.

"Sweet dreams."

"You too."

They fell asleep quickly, and for the first time in a long while, both of them slept sounder than they ever had.

***

Kate woke slowly, blinking as she took in her surroundings, momentarily disoriented. Then, as she shifted slightly, she realized Haley was curled against her, sleeping soundly. For a quiet, precious moment, Kate let herself take it in, feeling the warmth of Haley's body nestled against hers. She couldn't help but smile, pulling Haley just a little closer and marveling at how beautiful she looked, like a sleeping angel.

Unable to resist, Kate brushed a soft kiss against Haley's lips, hoping to wake her gently. Haley stirred, her eyes fluttering open just as Kate leaned in for a second kiss. But this time, she felt the gentle, unexpected brush of Haley's tongue, and a jolt of surprise ran through her. Instinctively, she wrapped her arms tighter around Haley's body, pulling her even closer. The kiss deepened, slow and warm, filling the quiet morning with an unspoken connection that made Kate's heart race. In that moment, the world beyond their embrace faded away, leaving only the soft, steady rhythm of their closeness, a feeling so rare and precious Kate could hardly believe it was real.

But the moment was short-lived. A loud knock on the door shattered the intimacy, startling them both. Tangled in each other and the blankets, they scrambled awkwardly off the small bed, tumbling to the floor in a breathless heap. The sudden chill of the morning air, the hard landing, and the relentless knock brought them crashing back to reality, pulling them abruptly out of the passion they'd been lost in just moments before.

"You two alive in there?" came Charles's voice from outside.

Kate scrambled to her feet, still brushing off the awkwardness. "Yeah, we're fine. Just a second." She rushed to the door, opening it to find Charles standing there with a thermos of coffee and a basket of homemade peach scones, a grin plastered on his face as he took in the scene.

"Wow, Kate. I've never seen you sleep in this late," he remarked, one eyebrow raised in amusement.

"Guess I was really out," Kate replied, trying to smooth her hair and maintain some semblance of composure.

Charles's gaze swept over the room, lingering on the blankets strewn across the floor and the rumpled bed. A smirk tugged at his mouth as he put two and two together. "Looks like y'all figured out a way to stay warm," he noted, the knowing look in his eyes unmistakable.

Haley, still half-asleep and sprawled on the floor, groggily reached out. "Coffee...please...thank you," she mumbled, rubbing her eyes.

Charles chuckled, handing her a cup. "You're welcome," he said with a grin. "So, what's on the agenda for you two today?"

Kate paused, a bit taken aback, but Haley jumped in first. "Actually, I think I'll tag along with Kate today. Might as well get a feel for the ranch."

Charles's eyebrow shot up, clearly surprised. "So... you're planning to ride out with Kate?"

"Yep," Haley replied, rising from the floor and taking a sip of coffee. "You never know where inspiration might strike."

Charles looked back and forth between them, still wrapping his head around this unexpected turn. "Alright then. And you're good with this?" he asked, eyeing Kate.

Kate gave a slight smirk. "I'll keep her in one piece."

Their eyes held for a brief, unspoken moment before both quickly looked away. Charles, ever the observer, ambled toward the door, tossing Kate a playful wink as he passed. Kate rolled her eyes, then shut the door behind him, leaving Haley alone to eagerly dive into the basket of fresh scones.

Kate watched her, amused. "Let me guess—you didn't pack anything remotely suitable for riding?"

"Mmm, no," Haley admitted, mid-bite, then paused thoughtfully. "But I bet you're the type who could build a fire out of nothing."

Kate gave her a puzzled look. "What?"

"I once knew this girl who'd say she wanted a husband who could build a fire from nothing," Haley explained, leaning back, looking half amused and half serious.

Kate raised an eyebrow, doubtful. "A fire from nothing? You mean just... poof?"

Haley shrugged. "I guess it made her feel like she'd be safe in a crisis. Someone who could handle anything."

Kate smirked. "Sounds ridiculous to me," she replied flatly, heading over to the closet.

She began pulling out warm clothes and tossing them onto the bed. As she turned back, she noticed Haley watching her intently, a hint of curiosity in her eyes.

"I can start a fire from nothing," Kate said with a smirk, "but I would never put us in a situation where I had to."

Haley smiled, her eyes warm. Kate turned back to the closet to grab more clothes, and a smile crept onto her face as well.

Chapter 14

Haley stood bundled up in layers, looking slightly apprehensive as Kate expertly saddled her horse. Louie, Kate's horse, was already saddled and waiting calmly. Kate led Haley's horse, Bucky, over and gave him a gentle pat on the neck.

"Now, Bucky," Kate said playfully, giving the horse an affectionate rub, "this is Haley, and she's going to be riding you today. Be nice."

Haley raised an eyebrow, her skepticism apparent. "You're really giving me a horse named Bucky?"

Kate shrugged, still petting Bucky. "He doesn't know what it means."

"But he understood everything you just said?" Haley asked, clearly unconvinced.

Kate grinned, grabbing a small mounting stool and setting it beside the horse. "Probably not."

Haley's pride kicked in as she watched Kate casually step back, crossing her arms. "I'm not a total amateur," she declared, moving determinedly to mount Bucky without the stool.

Kate raised her brows, taking a step back with a smile. "Oh, excuse me. By all means."

Haley grabbed the saddle, trying to swing her leg up. But her bundled-up layers made every movement feel like a struggle, her motions restricted and awkward.

"Ugh...this isn't exactly Pilates-friendly," Haley muttered, her frustration starting to show.

"Uh-huh, that must be it," Kate said, her amusement barely concealed.

Looking like a determined but overstuffed marshmallow, Haley kept trying to hoist herself onto Bucky. Kate stood back, clearly enjoying the show.

"Haley," Kate finally said, gently, "there's no shame in using the stool. It's just me here—no one to impress."

"I'm not trying to impress you," Haley shot back, still struggling.

Kate smirked, folding her arms. "Good, because you're definitely not."

Haley sighed, giving in. "Fine. Get me the stool."

Kate's grin widened as she placed the stool beside Bucky. Haley stepped up, and as she did, they found themselves unexpectedly close, face to face. Haley cleared her throat, muttering, "It's these clothes. They limit my range of motion."

"Right," Kate replied, a playful glint in her eye. Before Haley could react, Kate leaned in, brushing a quick, soft kiss on her lips. It was brief, but enough to make Haley's cheeks flush and a small smile tug at the corner of her mouth.

With the help of the stool, Haley finally settled into the saddle, and Kate walked over to her own horse, mounting Louie with practiced ease, her own smile lingering as they prepared to ride together.

"Alright, showoff," Haley muttered, rolling her eyes.

Kate just chuckled. "Ready to ride?"

Kate led Haley across a gentle slope to a spot where a massive oak tree stood, its branches stretching wide against the snowy landscape. The tree looked timeless, a sturdy presence that had witnessed years of seasons coming and going. Kate swung off Louie and gave him a gentle pat before leading him closer to the tree. She turned back, extending a hand to help Haley down from Bucky's saddle.

As Haley slid down, her footing was a bit unsteady, and she instinctively reached for Kate's arm. They stood there for a brief moment, just inches apart, and their eyes met. For a second, it felt like the world had stilled around them, the quiet snow-muted sounds, the crisp cold air, and the closeness.

Kate cleared her throat, breaking the moment and gesturing toward the base of the oak. "See this tree? It's my favorite spot. There's a bit of a surprise here."

"A surprise?" Haley raised an eyebrow, intrigued. "What, did you carve a secret message for your future wife or something?" She grinned, adding, "Or is this where the ranch hides its Starbucks?"

Kate laughed, shaking her head as she knelt down, brushing snow away from the tree's bark until a set of carved initials appeared. "Not quite. I found this a few years back." She glanced up at Haley, her smile softening. "It's your grandparents' initials."

Haley knelt down beside Kate, brushing her gloved fingers over the bark as she uncovered a set of carved initials within a heart: "JH + LH." She traced them delicately, as if the initials might dissolve under her touch.

"Oh my God," Haley whispered, her voice thick with emotion. "These are Meemaw and Pawpaw's." She paused, running her fingertips over each letter. "I had no idea they left something here."

Kate nodded, her voice soft. "I found it not long after I started working here. It's like they wanted to leave a piece of themselves behind, something tied to this place they loved so much."

Haley swallowed, struggling to keep her composure. "They did love it. This ranch... it was everything to them."

Kate's hand moved to her shoulder, a quiet gesture of comfort. "There's more," she said, her tone gentle. She cleared away a bit more snow, revealing a second carving—another set of initials.

Haley's breath hitched as she recognized them: "JH & KH." Her parents' initials.

Her eyes brimmed with tears as she traced them, memories flooding her mind. "My mom and dad..." she whispered, her voice breaking. She took a shaky breath, trying to hold it together, but the weight of their absence pressed down on her.

Kate sat beside her, watching her carefully. "I thought you'd want to see this. I know how hard it's been, coming back here. But they're... they're part of this place, Haley."

Haley looked up at her, eyes glistening. "It's so much harder than I thought. Being here... it's like I can feel them everywhere." She shook her head, standing up quickly. "I... I need a minute."

Without another word, she turned, walking briskly toward Bucky. She climbed up onto her horse, her movements almost mechanical, driven by the need to escape before her emotions overwhelmed her.

Kate watched her go, understanding Haley's need for space but feeling a pang of worry. After a moment, she mounted Louie and quietly followed at a distance, her gaze never leaving Haley's retreating figure as they headed back toward the ranch in silence.

Chapter 15

As Haley rode back toward the barn alone, a heavy silence pressed down on her. The warmth of the rising sun touched everything around her, casting a gentle glow over the familiar landscape, but it felt muted, almost hollow. She'd left Kate behind at the old oak tree—the place where, just moments earlier, her fingers had brushed across her parents' initials carved into the bark, weathered but unmistakable. Seeing those letters, faded yet enduring, had stirred something sharp and painful, cutting through the fragile peace she'd tried so hard to hold onto.

Her mind drifted back to the summers she'd spent here as a kid, running wild through the fields, learning how to ride, her father's hand steadying hers on the reins, her mother laughing softly as she watched from the barn. Those were the golden days, when the ranch was more than just land and buildings; it was a heartbeat, the center of her family. She could almost hear her mother's voice in the wind, calling her home for dinner, or the steady murmur of her father as he tended to the horses. Those memories wrapped around her, familiar yet suffocating, reminding her of what she'd lost.

Since the accident, being here felt like walking through a maze of ghosts. She'd avoided the ranch for so long, pushing down the guilt and grief, afraid to face the reminders of a life that no longer existed. Now, everywhere she looked, she was surrounded by fragments of the past, as if the land itself refused to let her forget. It was beautiful, but it was also a weight—a constant reminder that she was living in a place built on memories and loss.

The closer she got to the barn, the lighter the ache in her chest grew. She loved this place, but that love came with an unbearable cost. She couldn't shake the feeling that being here meant stepping into shoes she'd never truly fit. Her parents had poured their souls into this ranch, building it up, dreaming big dreams for it. And now, standing here, she couldn't help but feel like an outsider trespassing on sacred ground, forever trying to live up to an impossible legacy.

As she reached the barn, Haley slowed Bucky to a stop, letting her gaze drift over the familiar lines of the building, the way the wood gleamed softly in the golden light. She should feel at home, anchored in the place that had raised her, but all she felt was a hollow ache, a yearning for something she couldn't name.

She dismounted, her boots hitting the ground with a soft thud, the silence around her suddenly too loud, too empty. She led Bucky into the barn, her movements mechanical, trying to ground herself in the routine, but the memories kept slipping in, unbidden and relentless. Her parents' voices echoed faintly in her mind, mingling with the familiar smells of hay and leather, drawing her deeper into the past she wished she could escape.

After securing Bucky's reins, Haley took a shaky breath and stepped outside, needing the open air to clear her head. She leaned against the barn door, staring out over the vast expanse of land, her gaze lost somewhere in the distance. She'd come back to help, to keep the ranch alive, but each day here felt like peeling back layers of a wound that refused to heal. She wanted to run, to escape the weight of it all, but something kept her rooted in place, a stubborn loyalty that wouldn't let her leave.

Haley closed her eyes, feeling the cool morning breeze brush against her skin, a bittersweet reminder of all the things she could never truly leave behind.

As Haley leaned against the barn door, staring out over the land that held so much of her past, a quiet clarity began to settle in her chest, mingling with the ache of old memories. She'd come back with every intention of finding a way to hold on to the ranch, to keep her parents' legacy alive. But now, standing there, she understood what she'd been avoiding for so long, the truth that had been pressing at the edges of her heart since she first set foot back on this land.

They couldn't keep it.

No amount of love, loyalty, or sacrifice could change the reality. The ranch, with all its memories, was a weight they couldn't bear on their own. Haley resigned herself to the fact that she'd have to tell Charles. She'd have to break the news that would crush them both—they couldn't make this work; they'd have to let it go. Haley took a deep breath, feeling the finality of her decision settle over her like a heavy blanket. She knew it wouldn't be easy; telling Charles would be one of the hardest things she'd ever have to do. But he deserved the truth, and it was time they faced it together. They'd have to sell the ranch, let someone else take over this land and its legacy.

Gathering herself, Haley pushed off from the barn door and made her way across the yard. The familiar crunch of gravel under her boots felt like a heartbeat, steady and grounding, even as her own pulse quickened with the weight of what lay ahead. She needed to find Charles, to have the conversation they'd both dreaded. Taking one last look at the vast stretch of land before her, she turned and set off to find him, preparing herself to let go of the only home she'd ever known.

***

Kate had been following behind Haley on the ride back to the barn, close enough to see her silhouette against the morning light but far enough to give her space. She'd sensed the heaviness in Haley's expression when they'd paused at the old oak tree, and something told her that Haley needed a moment alone. So, she'd hung back, letting her own thoughts wander as they both made their way back toward the barn.

Now, as Kate entered the quiet structure, a faint unease began to settle over her. She led Louie into his stall, glancing around for any sign of Haley. The barn was silent, only the soft rustle of hay and the occasional nicker from a horse breaking the stillness. Bucky was already secured, unsaddled and fed, a sign that Haley had been here. But now, there was no sign of her.

"Haley?" she called out, her voice carrying softly in the calm morning air. She paused, waiting for a reply, but the silence seemed almost too thick, too still, as if the barn itself held its breath.

A sense of worry stirred in Kate's chest as she stepped back outside, squinting into the bright light of late morning. She scanned the yard, searching for any movement, hoping to see Haley somewhere nearby. But the ranch lay empty, the fields stretching out under the sun, quiet and untouched.

Leaning against the barn door, Kate's gaze lingered on the open land, a faint frown tugging at her lips. Haley had slipped away without a word, vanishing into the brightness of the morning, leaving Kate with a strange, unsettled feeling and a quiet sense of loss.

Chapter 16

Kate found Haley sitting at the dining room table, surrounded by paperwork. She stood just out of sight, hidden behind the doorway in the hall, trying to drum up the courage to confront her about what had happened out in the pasture. But before she could make a move, Charles swooped in, cutting off her chance.

"So?" Charles asked, his tone light, though he was clearly fishing for good news. "Did you find inspiration today with Kate?"

Haley let out a frustrated sigh. "No. There's no saving it. We have to sell, Charles. I've been through this a million times."

Charles stiffened, his face falling. "Haley, this is our home."

"That's the problem," Haley replied, shaking her head. "You're putting all this sentimental value on a business. You can't see what's so obviously clear to anyone with a calculator."

"It's our family home," Charles insisted, his voice growing more urgent. "After they died, this was your home."

"This was never my home," Haley snapped, her frustration boiling over. "You love it, I get that. But I never belonged here."

"That's not true," Charles countered. "You loved this place once. You belong here as much as you do in San Francisco."

"I don't know where I belong!" Haley shot back, her voice breaking. "Okay? Maybe I don't belong anywhere."

Kate held her breath as she looked on from her spot just beyond the doorway, her hands clenched tightly at her sides. Haley's words hung heavy in the air, and she could feel the sting of them, even as an observer. She hadn't expected to overhear a conversation like this tonight, but now she was rooted to the spot, unable to walk away.

Charles's voice softened, though Kate could hear the hurt in it. "This place has always been a part of you, Haley. No matter where you've been, it's always been here, waiting for you."

Haley pushed her chair back and stood, a look of exhaustion shadowing her face. "You don't get it, Charles," she said, running a hand through her hair. "You look at this place and see family, roots. I look at it, and... it just reminds me of things I don't have anymore. Of people I've lost. I can't stand this heaviness in my chest."

Kate's heart ached, a pang of empathy mixing with an urge to step in and say something, anything, to soften the sharp edges of Haley's words.

"But we're still here, Haley," Charles said, his voice low and steady. "Meemaw, me...we're still your family. That doesn't disappear just because life got complicated. You belong here as much as I do."

Haley's shoulders slumped, her defiance fading. "I wish I felt that, Charles. But the city... it's simpler. It doesn't ask things of me like this place does." Her gaze drifted around the ranch, her expression tinged with something close to regret.

Here, everything was charged with memories and expectations, layers of history she could feel in every fencepost, every stretch of field. It was as if the land itself held the weight of her parents' dreams, waiting for her to carry them on. But in the city, she was just Haley. She could slip into the rhythm of busy streets, the anonymity of crowds, a life that didn't demand she look too closely at who she was or what she was running from.

"In the city," she continued, her voice soft, "I can breathe without feeling like I'm letting anyone down. There's no land to keep up, no past trying to pull me back. I can go to work, lose myself in tasks that are just... tasks. No ghosts lingering in the walls, no legacy waiting to be upheld."

She glanced back at Charles, her expression conflicted. "Here, it's like every corner, every sunrise, is asking something of me. To be better, to be stronger, to hold it all together for everyone who came before us. It's... overwhelming. In the city, I don't have to feel that weight. I don't have to live up to anything but my own expectations." She looked down, her voice barely a whisper. "I'm sorry."

There was a long silence, one so thick Kate could feel it in her chest. She was seconds away from stepping out, from making her presence known, but something held her back.

Charles took a deep breath, his hands resting heavily on the table. "I hope you realize something," he said quietly. "In the city, there's no one who really knows who you are. Your sense of self gets lost, piece by piece. Who's going to truly love the real Haley if you're denying the parts of yourself that are too painful to feel? This place, these people—we're a part of you. And you can't run away from our love forever."

Haley looked away, her face unreadable. "I wish it were that simple," she whispered, almost to herself. Then, more firmly, she added, "Love isn't going to pay the bills." Without another word, she turned and walked out of the room, leaving Charles sitting alone in the soft glow of the dining room light.

Kate stepped back, allowing Haley to pass without noticing her, feeling the weight of everything she'd just overheard. She looked back at Charles, who sat at the table, staring at the empty chair across from him, lost in thought.

***

Haley walked over to the fireplace, her gaze settling on the old photos lined up along the mantle. She reached out to one of them, her fingers lightly tracing the edges of a framed picture of her and her parents, the three of them smiling on a bright summer day she could barely remember.

Behind her, Kate's quiet voice broke the silence. "How old were you?" she asked softly.

Startled, Haley turned, the photo still in her hands. "Here?" She held it up for Kate to see.

Kate shook her head gently, her expression filled with understanding. "No... I meant when they passed. The accident."

Haley's face tightened, her voice dropping. "They died three weeks before my thirteenth birthday." Her words hung heavy in the room, weighed down by years of pain. "I thought getting out of here would fix everything," Haley said, staring at the photo in her hand.

"Did it?" Kate asked gently.

Haley gave a bitter laugh. "No. That took thousands of dollars of therapy."

Kate smiled slightly. "Oh, well then you're totally fine now."

Haley smirked, shaking her head. "Ha. Ha."

Kate's expression softened. "I don't think you hate this place. I think you love it here. But it reminds you of your parents. And that's why you never come. It makes you miss them. And that's painful."

Haley's eyes hardened as she set the photo back on the mantle.

Kate stepped forward, crossing the room to stand beside her. She looked at the photo of Haley as a child. "This girl right here?" Kate said, her voice quiet. "I saw her today when you were riding."

"That girl had her parents," Haley said bitterly, her voice cracking.

"I know it's hard," Kate said, her tone gentle. "There's pain for you here, but there's joy too."

"Great speech, Kate," Haley said, her voice dripping with sarcasm. "Really. Maybe you should take your own advice?"

"We're not talking about me," Kate replied, her posture stiffening.

"Then let's talk about you," Haley shot back. "You can stand here and judge my life and choices, but you're too stubborn to call your family?"

"That's different..." Kate started.

"Yes, it is," Haley cut her off, her voice sharp. "You still have parents to call. They may not be perfect, but they're here, and you could at least try. I can't—I'll never be able to tell mine how much I love them or vent about my terrible dating life or share if I'm actually in love. They're gone, and you don't get to stand here and give me these feel-good speeches about family and belonging."

With those words hanging heavy in the air, Haley turned and stormed out, leaving Kate stunned and motionless. Kate leaned against the mantle, eyes drifting down to the family photos, her thoughts tangled and weighed down by Haley's words.

Haley stepped outside, her phone pressed tightly to her ear as she dialed Steve, her breath visible in the cold night air.

"I need a flight out tonight," she said, her voice tense, barely concealing her frustration.

"That's impossible, Haley," Steve replied, his voice crackling through the weak connection. "It's not exactly a major airport. The closest I can do is tomorrow afternoon."

Haley let out a sharp sigh. "Fine. Whatever. Just get me out of here as soon as you can."

Steve hesitated, sensing her tension. "You okay?" His voice softened, filled with genuine concern.

Haley's voice cracked slightly, but she forced herself to keep it steady. "Yeah. Just... dumb family stuff." She paused, swallowing back the sting in her throat. "Please just send the flight info when you have it."

"Alright," Steve replied gently, sensing he shouldn't press further. "Take care, Haley."

"Thanks," she whispered, barely audible. She hung up the call and stood there, phone in hand, staring out into the vast darkness of the ranch. The night was still and quiet, the sky stretching endlessly above her, stars piercing through the black in cold pinpricks of light.

Haley leaned her forehead against one of the porch posts, overcome with emotion as memories and the weight of the night bore down on her. Her shoulders shook as silent tears slid down her cheeks, her body trembling with a sadness she hadn't allowed herself to feel in so long. In the stillness, the ranch seemed to hold its breath, as if sharing her sorrow in its own quiet, unspoken way.

**

Kate stood just inside the ranch's front window, barely out of sight but close enough to catch glimpses of Haley, her silhouette illuminated by the faint glow of the porch light. Through the glass, she watched Haley press her phone to her ear, her shoulders tense and voice muffled by the barrier between them. It was late, and the night wrapped itself around the ranch in a thick silence that made Haley's body language all the more readable.

Kate's heart tightened as she saw Haley's expression shift — her brows pulling together, jaw clenched. She could imagine the conversation, and could almost hear Haley's clipped, frustrated tone. Then, suddenly, Haley's face softened, her shoulders dropping as she seemed to listen to whatever the person on the other end was saying. A flash of vulnerability crossed Haley's face, and Kate felt an urge to step outside, to close the space between them, but she stayed put, hands gripping the edge of the curtain.

When Haley finally hung up, she didn't move, just stared into the empty night, her figure casting a long shadow across the porch. Kate watched as Haley leaned forward, resting her head against the porch post, her shoulders starting to shake.

A pang of helplessness shot through Kate. She knew Haley had come here with her defenses high, ready to tackle the ranch problem head-on, and seeing her now, unraveling under the weight of it all, felt painfully intimate. She wanted to rush out there, to comfort her, but something held her back — maybe Haley needed this moment alone, or maybe Kate didn't know what to say.

Kate's gaze softened, her own breath catching as she saw Haley swipe at a tear, trying to compose herself. Kate's fingers twitched at her side, aching to reach out, to bridge whatever gap had grown between them. The ranch felt vast and quiet around her, like it was holding onto secrets, and she realized that Haley was one of them — something raw and unresolved.

***

Meemaw and Charles sat at the breakfast table in solemn silence, the weight of the decision pressing down on them, as tangible as the chill morning air. The only sounds filling the room were the quiet clinking of silverware against the worn plates and the soft crackle of the fire that Meemaw had tended to earlier, though even its usual warmth felt muted today.

Haley's footsteps descended softly from the stairs, each one slow and tentative. She entered the room, noticing the heaviness in the air immediately, and took a deep breath before stepping forward. Charles looked up, his eyes meeting hers with a look she couldn't quite place—somewhere between apology and regret.

"Family meeting," Meemaw announced, breaking the silence with a tone that attempted to be steady but held a waver.

"Okay," Haley replied, her voice quiet, as she cautiously took a seat across from them, her gaze shifting between her brother and Meemaw.

Meemaw's expression grew even heavier as she turned to Haley, her weathered hands folded on the table in front of her. "Charles told me what you said last night," she began, her voice thick with resignation. "I know you tried really hard. But... we're going to take your advice and sell to the Berts."

Haley felt the words like a physical blow, her heart sinking under the weight of them. The ache in her chest surprised her, and she reached out, her fingers wrapping around Meemaw's hand, seeking comfort even as she struggled to offer it. "I'm sorry," she murmured, her voice soft but sincere, her gaze moving from Meemaw to Charles. "I really did try. I just couldn't..." Her voice broke off, the words failing her.

"It's not your fault, honey," Meemaw replied, squeezing Haley's hand, her tone filled with a quiet reassurance that carried years of understanding. "We know you tried. Sometimes things just don't work out the way we want them to, no matter how much we wish otherwise."

Haley nodded, biting down the surge of emotion threatening to overtake her, struggling to keep her composure. Her gaze dropped to the table, searching for something to anchor herself, when a sudden thought made her look up. "Wait, where's Kate?" she asked, the absence suddenly feeling like another weight.

"Kate?" Charles echoed, looking slightly confused.

"Yeah," Haley pressed. "Isn't she a part of this too?"

Meemaw answered. "Left early this morning for Fox Springs."

"Oh," Haley said, feeling a pang of disappointment.

Charles glanced at her. "I imagine you'll be on your way before she comes back."

"Yes," Haley confirmed, though the thought of leaving unsettled her. After a pause, she added, "But I was thinking... maybe I can come back after the holidays, when you find a new place. Help you move in and get set up."

Meemaw's face brightened slightly. "Oh, that would be nice."

Standing up, Meemaw pulled Haley into a warm, comforting hug. "It's been good having you here," she whispered softly in Haley's ear. "I still believe in you."

As Meemaw left the room, Charles sat quietly, watching Haley sip her coffee.

"I'm sorry I couldn't come up with a plan," Haley said, her voice heavy with guilt.

Charles shook his head. "I'm just glad you came home."

Haley's eyes softened. "You and Meemaw are all I have."

"Please come around more," Charles said earnestly.

"I will," Haley promised. "I realized how much I miss everyone and that maybe I do have a little country girl in me, more than I realized."

Charles gave a small smile. "What are you going to do?" Haley asked.

"Not sure," Charles replied with a sigh. "Once I get things settled here, I'll decide."

They both stood up from the table, and Charles pulled Haley into a tight hug. The weight of their shared loss hung between them, but there was a sense of comfort in their embrace.

"We've lost a lot," Charles said quietly, "but we have so much."

"I know," Haley whispered. "Love you, bro."

Haley sat at her desk, her fingers idly scrolling through ranches and rolling hills photos on her computer screen, though her mind was a thousand miles away. It had been a week since she returned from Hollis Hills, back in the polished setting of her high-rise office, but the familiar surroundings didn't bring her any comfort. If anything, she felt more disconnected here than ever. The wide, open land of the ranch, the warmth of her family, and those last moments with Kate haunted her thoughts. Every sleek glass wall, every humming fluorescent light felt foreign now, as if she had slipped back into someone else's life.

The city that used to thrill her, the pulse of her ambition, the drive to succeed—it all felt strangely hollow. Her gaze drifted over the view outside her window, skyscrapers and bustling streets sprawling out below, but they were nothing compared to the rolling hills and open sky of the ranch. Here, life had rhythm and order, but out there? It had meaning. She missed Hollis Hills more than she cared to admit. Every time she tried to focus, her mind drifted back to that early morning ride, the quiet tension with Kate, the way they'd both tried to ignore what was simmering under the surface. An ache had taken root, a gnawing emptiness she couldn't quite name, as if she'd left something vital behind.

The usual hum of the office seemed muted, the bustling activity somehow distant. A heavy sigh escaped her as she tried to shake off the sadness pressing down on her chest. She'd worked so hard to build this life—her career, her accomplishments, her independence—and yet, for the first time, it felt incomplete. She couldn't remember the last time she'd felt so... restless.

A knock at the door snapped her out of her reverie, and she looked up as Steve, her ever-loyal assistant, poked his head into the office, breaking her train of thought.

"Still haven't heard from Eric?" he asked, stepping fully inside and folding his arms.

"Nope," Haley replied, her voice distant. "He's been in meetings since I got back." She tried to sound casual, but there was a note of frustration she couldn't hide. She needed clarity, something to ground her.

Steve, always the optimist, flashed a reassuring smile. "That's a good sign, right?" he offered, clearly trying to lift her spirits. "He's probably working out all the details so it's perfect when he gets back to you."

Haley forced a smile, but it didn't reach her eyes. "Maybe," she said, glancing back at her screen. Another photo of a sprawling green field, dotted with wildflowers, popped up, and she felt a pang. It was strange to feel homesick for a place she'd spent so many years avoiding.

"Maybe," Haley said again, but her heart wasn't in it.

Just then, her phone buzzed on the desk. She glanced down at the screen, raising an eyebrow. It was Eric.

"Speak of the devil," she murmured, picking up the phone. "Eric wants me upstairs immediately."

Steve shot her an encouraging grin. "Moment of truth!" he said, his energy unflagging. Haley returned a small smile and stood up, smoothing down her skirt as she gathered herself.

As she made her way to the elevator, Haley tried to summon the thrill she used to feel for these moments, the charge that usually buzzed through her when a big decision was on the line. She could almost hear the faint echo of her own excitement from a time when this job meant everything to her. But now, it felt strangely hollow.

CHRISTMAS AT THE RANCH

The elevator doors opened, and she stepped inside, pressing the button for the top floor. The soft hum of the elevator vibrated through her, but her mind was far away, drifting back to Hollis Hills. She could still feel the crispness of the ranch air, the warmth of the fireplace, and the way her family had looked at her that last morning—a mixture of love and acceptance... and maybe a little sadness. It lingered, a sharp contrast to the sterile world of glass and steel she stood in now. Yet, even here, she couldn't escape the thought of Kate—the soft curve of her lips, the fleeting warmth of her touch. The memory was as vivid and persistent as the ranch itself, an unwelcome reminder of everything she'd left behind.

She wished, for the thousandth time, that she had stayed just a little longer, long enough to say goodbye properly. Maybe that was it. The way they'd left things felt unfinished, like there was something unsaid lingering between them, something she couldn't quite shake.

As the elevator rose, her pulse quickened, and she took a deep breath, steadying herself. This was her moment—what she had worked so hard for. But why did it suddenly feel so distant, like she was stepping into someone else's life?

When the doors opened, Haley squared her shoulders, ready to face whatever awaited her in Eric's office.

Eric was standing by the large windows, his gaze fixed on the city skyline as the early afternoon light cast a warm glow over the room. Haley knocked softly on the door, her heartbeat quickening with a mix of nervous excitement and anticipation. The familiar office air, filled with the scent of coffee and faint hints of polished wood, suddenly felt heavy. She forced a small smile, hoping it hid the apprehension flickering beneath.

"Come on in!" Eric called, turning to face her with an infectious grin that reached his eyes. He held an envelope in his hand, extending it toward her like he was revealing a prize.

Haley stepped inside, the click of her heels muffled by the thick carpet. Her nerves prickled, creeping in as she approached his desk, her mind racing with possibilities. Eric's wide smile only fueled her curiosity and unease.

"Hales," Eric said, practically beaming. "We sold."

Haley's eyes widened in shock, a genuine smile breaking across her face. "We did? That's amazing!"

"It is," Eric agreed, his excitement mirroring hers. He walked over to her, still holding the envelope, his grip firm but his tone light with pride. "And this... is for you." He offered the envelope with a sense of ceremony, his expression warm and full of unspoken appreciation.

Haley took the envelope from his hand, her fingers trembling slightly as she opened it. Her jaw dropped when she saw the amount inside.

"Oh my God," she whispered, her voice barely audible.

"I know, right?" Eric grinned, clearly enjoying the moment. "You earned it. We all earned it. Your presentation sealed the deal."

"This is so exciting!" Haley exclaimed, throwing her arms around Eric in a spontaneous hug.

"Right on, consensual hugging," Eric said, patting her back. "The retreat was a dud, so you really saved us."

Haley pulled back, her brow furrowed. "The retreat was a dud? I thought that was a great idea."

"Right?" Eric said, shaking his head. "Me too. But when we got there, it was all brunches, parties, and champagne. Just constant pampering."

Haley blinked. "And that was... bad?"

"Yeah," Eric said, a little exasperated. "I wanted to rough it. Sleep under the stars. Rope cows and, like, ride horses. Tough stuff. Rugged man bonding. Like Brokeback Mountain, you know?"

Haley gave him a curious look. "Um, Eric... have you actually seen Brokeback Mountain?"

"Just the first half," Eric said, nodding enthusiastically. "But it looked cool as hell. Just some macho guys out in the wilderness. Becoming best friends."

Haley bit back a smile. "Mmm. Hmm. That's... yep."

"Oh, but there was one thing that was actually really cool," Eric continued, his face lighting up. "They brought in this energy healer, and she did a Chilean butterfly naming party or something."

"A naming ceremony?" Haley asked, a sudden thought striking her. "Wait. Masonry?"

"Yeah, that's her!" Eric said, pointing at her. "You've heard of her? She's amazing. That was the only time I felt really connected. Out there by the fire, with just the sounds of nature. No screens, no distractions, you know?"

Haley nodded slowly. "I do know. I know exactly what you mean. Did the universe give you a name?"

"Totally," Eric said, his voice full of anticipation.

Haley raised an eyebrow, waiting for the big reveal.

"And it was..." she prompted.

"Eric," he said, mimicking an explosion with his hands. "I know, right? Mind. Blown. I really felt my own power that night."

"Right," Haley said, trying not to laugh. "Of course."

"Anyways, Masonry is a genius," Eric continued, pacing excitedly. "She has, like, three million Snapback followers. Dude, you should bring her on to do some social media stuff. If you decide to stay, of course."

Haley froze. "Stay?"

Eric nodded, looking at her seriously. "Yeah. With that check, you won't have to work here, or anywhere, honestly. You can do whatever you want."

The realization hit Haley like a ton of bricks. She looked down at the check in her hand, her mind racing.

"Oh my God," she whispered, her eyes widening. "Oh my God, Eric. You're right!"

Chapter 17

The air in the room grew thick with tension, weighing down every breath. Charles, Bert, and Bert Jr. sat around the table, the silence heavy between them as they reviewed the final paperwork, the crackle of the fire in the next room, the only soft sound punctuating the tension.

Charles's gaze drifted to the familiar details of the house he'd known all his life—the worn grain of the oak table, the faded portrait on the wall of his parents beaming proudly beside the barn. He clenched his jaw, feeling the sting of helplessness claw at him.

"Everything we discussed is in here?" Charles asked, forcing his voice steady as he glanced up at Bert.

"Lawyers checked it all yesterday," Bert replied smoothly, flipping through the pages with an air of smug satisfaction. "All you gotta do is have your Meemaw sign her name, then I'll take it to the lawyer's office before they close today.

Bert Jr. leaned back with a smirk, his eyes glinting with arrogance. "Where's Kate?"

Charles shot him a sharp glare. "We still have Christmas hayrides to run."

Bert Jr. scoffed, his smirk widening. "Not for long."

Charles's fists clenched under the table. "You can't take away our Christmas spirit," he snapped. "We'll keep doing them for the joy of the season until the very end. You don't own this ranch until the bank says you do!"

The words were like a declaration, a stubborn refusal to let them strip away the heart of the ranch so easily. He shot up from his seat, the old chair creaking as he did. "Alright, Bert. Let's go have her sign it."

As they moved toward the door, Bert gave a smug smile. "Thank you, Charlie," he said, his tone mockingly polite. "I'll give y'all until the end of the year to vacate—my Christmas gift to you."

"You're a regular Santa Claus," Charles muttered under his breath.

Bert Jr. snickered. "Do as many little hayrides as you can."

As they walked toward the door, the sound of horns honking in the distance caught their attention.

Now what. Charles thought as he moved quickly to the front door, flinging it open to see Walter's truck speeding down the driveway toward the house.

***

Charles bolted outside, Meemaw already standing on the porch.

"What are you doing, Walter?" Bert yelled, walking down the steps. "Get this hunk of junk out of my way!"

Walter just smiled and waved as Haley and Masonry hopped out of the truck. Masonry, dressed in her signature eclectic outfit for the cold weather, sported a flower crown on her head.

"It's Haley!" Charles shouted. "And I'm not sure who that is..."

Meemaw grinned knowingly. "Here she comes."

Haley marched straight up to Bert, snatching the contract out of his hands. Without a word, she tore them up right in his face, tossing the shredded pieces into the air. They fluttered around like confetti, carried away by the wind.

Meemaw let out a triumphant laugh. "Haha! That's what I wanted to see!"

Bert's face turned red with rage. "Hey! What do you think you're doing?"

"We're not selling," Haley said firmly, her eyes locked on his.

Masonry, horrified by the paper mess, frantically began picking up the torn pieces. "Haley! The environment!"

"Sorry, Masonry," Haley said, a little sheepish. "I was going for a whole... you know, dramatic thing."

Charles was still trying to catch up. "Haley, what are you doing? And who is that?"

Meemaw stood by a knowing smile on her face. "You were right, Meemaw!" Haley called over to her.

Masonry stood up, feeling the energy of the place. "That's our new energy healer and social media director," Haley explained casually.

Bert, bewildered, asked, "Your whatta?"

"Sorry, Bert," Haley said sweetly. "That's none of your business since you don't own this place. And as of this moment, you're officially trespassing."

"Tell that to the bank, honey," Bert snarled.

"Oh, I just did," Haley said with a smirk. "I stopped by there first and paid off all our debt." She turned to Meemaw, smiling. "Then I went to the lawyer's office. They should be contacting you shortly." She deferred to Meemaw with a grin. "Would you do the honors?"

Meemaw stepped forward, looking at Bert and his son with satisfaction. "Now, Bert and mini-Bert, get off my ranch."

Bert backed away toward his truck, his face contorted with frustration. "This isn't over."

"Oh yes it is," Haley said sweetly, her smile growing wider. "Honey."

Bert and Bert Jr. stormed off, slamming the doors of their truck. Walter gave them a cheerful wave as he drove off, while Masonry, still reeling from the torn paper, was doing her best to gather up the pieces.

Charles stared in disbelief. "You paid the bank?"

Haley nodded. "Yep. We're debt-free."

"Where'd you get the money?" he asked, still trying to process everything.

"Remember that huge project I was working on? Well, it paid off," Haley explained, smiling at him.

Meemaw's face beamed with pride. "You were right, Meemaw," Haley said softly.

Charles, still in shock, said, "Haley, you didn't have to."

"No, I didn't," Haley replied, her voice full of warmth. "I wanted to. Meemaw, I love this place." She turned to Charles. "And I belong here."

Meemaw pulled Haley into a big hug, both of them holding on tight.

"That's amazing, Haley. It really is," Charles said, though he couldn't help but glance over at Masonry. "But who is that?"

Haley followed his gaze. "Charles, let's be honest. You're not great at this ranching stuff. But you're brilliant with operations and numbers. If we have just enough of a 'Ranch Experience,' we can make so much more money. And I have an idea for that."

Masonry wandered over, her eyes shining with excitement. "You're right, Haley. It's perfect. The energy surrounding this place is like feminine power goodness. I feel it everywhere."

"There have been some really powerful women who have passed through here," Haley said, glancing at Meemaw.

Charles, still baffled, asked, "Who is this?"

Masonry grinned. "I'm Masonry."

Masonry winked and trotted over to Meemaw. "You are so authentic," she said, with admiration in her voice.

Meemaw smiled warmly. "Well, thank you. Why don't you come help me make a peach pie to celebrate?"

Masonry gasped. "Oh my God, peaches are my lunar cycle fruit!"

As they headed into the house, Charles turned back to Haley. "So, what's this big idea?"

"Outdoor experience retreat," Haley said with a grin. "Give overworked city slickers like me a break from the smog and their screens. They get to ride horses and play cowboy. Reconnect with nature."

Charles's eyes lit up. "That's a pretty great idea."

"Coming back here reminded me how beautiful this place is," Haley continued. "It reminded me of what's important. I want other people to feel that."

Charles smiled broadly. "So does that mean you're here to stay?"

"Yes," Haley said, feeling the truth of her words. "I'll have to get everything started. And of course, help you keep it going."

"Fantastic!" Charles exclaimed, pulling her into another hug. "It'll be nice to have you back. Kate will be thrilled."

Haley's eyes lit up. "Kate! Yes, I can't wait to tell her the good news! Wait... where is she?"

"She's getting ready for the Christmas hayride," Charles said with a grin.

"The hayride!" Haley's mind was racing. "I have an idea..." And with that, she dashed into the house.

Charles called after her, "What do I do with Masonry?"

Masonry appeared at his side, her eyes sparkling. "Wow. Your energy is like... wow."

Charles shifted uncomfortably. "Uh, thanks? Masonry, was it? Isn't that more of a skilled labor?"

Masonry gave him a dreamy smile. "And some say it is a dying art. You're funny. I wouldn't mind joining frequencies with you."

Charles blinked. "Um... okay."

***

Kate stood at the front of the hayride, her reindeer antlers perched on her head and her red nose glowing brightly, but beneath the festive costume, her heart felt heavy. She tried to stay in full storyteller mode, leading the guests in the tale of Rudolph the Red-Nosed Reindeer as the trailer slowly approached the first tableau. It was hard, though, knowing this might be her last Christmas hayride on the ranch. The thought of losing it all—the ranch, the traditions, and even Haley—left a hollow ache that made her wonder if she'd ever feel this kind of warmth again.

The chilly night air was filled with the sounds of jingling bells and joyful voices, and she let herself get lost in it for a moment.

"Jingle bells, jingle bells, jingle all the way, oh what fun it is to ride in a one-horse open sleeeigh!" Kate finished with practiced enthusiasm, her voice ringing out into the winter night. The group clapped and shook their bells in delight, and she let herself smile, just a bit, though it didn't quite reach her eyes.

"And now," Kate said, forcing a grin as they neared the next scene, "we have the story of Rudolph!" Her voice was cheerful, but her mind wandered. The crisp night air carried the faint scent of pine, and for a moment, she thought of Haley—of the way she laughed, her breath visible in the cold, and how her eyes sparkled when she teased her.

She swallowed and pushed down the longing that threatened to surface, masking it with the practiced smile she had perfected over the past few weeks. "Rudolph, everyone!" she said, waving her arm toward the glowing display ahead, but her heart wasn't in it.

The trailer slowed as they approached the first tableau: Santa Claus, standing tall and proud, holding a sign. But something was off. The sign wasn't part of the Rudolph story. Kate squinted, her smile faltering for a moment as she read the words:

This isn't the last Christmas hayride!

Kate hesitated, her heart skipping a beat, but quickly recovered. "Rudolph really wanted to be one of Santa's reindeer. He had a..." she glanced again at the sign, her voice wavering, "... red nose. All the reindeer used to make fun of him."

The guests chuckled, oblivious, but Kate's mind was racing. As the trailer moved to the next tableau, she was met with yet another surprise. There, on another sign, were words that made her breath catch. Her brow furrowed in confusion as she read:

I found inspiration to save the ranch!

Each word tugged at her heart, stirring hope she hadn't dared let herself feel.

Kate stammered slightly before picking up the story again. "Rudolph only wanted to help Santa and would do anything to spread Christmas cheer." Her voice wavered, but she continued as best she could.

As the hayride moved on, they arrived at the next part of the Rudolph story, but Kate's heart raced as she spotted yet another unexpected sign. Her eyes widened, and her breath caught when she read it:

I belong here...

A huge smile spread across her face, and she found herself rushing through the story, excitement bubbling up in her words. "So, uh, one Christmas, it was really foggy," she explained quickly, barely able to keep her composure, "and Santa saw Rudolph and said, 'I really need you to help me with your guiding light!'"

The tractor sped up, the final stretch in sight, but Kate could barely contain her joy. She turned back to the guests with a bright, beaming smile. "Alright, everyone, we're coming to the end of our hayride! Thank you so much for joining us tonight!"

The tractor pulled to a stop, and as the guests began packing up their bells and instruments, Kate waved them off, her mind spinning with the strange but thrilling signs. She was still processing it all when, out of the corner of her eye, she spotted Haley standing at the edge of the trailer, holding up a large sign.

The sign read: Can we try this again, Cowgrrl? Love, Joan.

Kate's breath hitched, her heart thudding in her chest. Before she could react, Haley stepped up to the trailer and climbed aboard. Kate, absorbed in tidying up a few last-minute hayride tasks, was caught off guard when the trailer shifted beneath her. Standing on an unsteady hay bale, she lost her balance, and with a sudden, unexpected jolt, she toppled straight into Haley's waiting arms.

They stood there, just inches apart, the world around them falling into a quiet stillness. Time seemed to pause, leaving just the two of them wrapped in that perfect moment. And then, without another word, they kissed—a movie-ending, heart-stopping kiss that made everything else disappear.

"You came back," Kate whispered, her forehead resting gently against Haley's, their breaths mingling in the crisp night air.

"Swooping in at the very last second and saving the day," Haley replied, her eyes shining with joy and relief, a spark of mischief lighting up her smile.

"The ranch is saved?" Kate asked, her voice still catching, as if she couldn't quite believe it.

Haley nodded, grinning wider. "I paid off the debt to the bank. And I have a great big idea—one that could make this place everything it deserves to be."

"Really?" Kate's eyes widened, a look of wonder and excitement filling them as she took in Haley's words.

"Yep," Haley said confidently, her gaze steady, full of hope and certainty.

A soft, radiant smile spread across Kate's face, her heart swelling with the overwhelming happiness that had felt like a distant dream only moments ago. "I took your suggestion and called my parents," she confessed, her voice quiet but proud.

Haley's face brightened, her whole expression lighting up as she took in this unexpected news. "You did? How did it go?" she asked eagerly, her voice softening with understanding, knowing just how much this had taken for Kate.

Kate exhaled, feeling the weight of it finally lifted. "Better than I expected," she admitted, her voice catching slightly. "It felt good. Really good."

"You were right," Kate said softly, her voice laced with warmth and a vulnerability she hadn't shown before. "I haven't stopped thinking about you. Not for a second."

"Me too," Haley replied, her heart racing. She quickly added with a shy smile, "But, you know, me thinking about you. Not me thinking about myself... that would be weird..."

Kate took a slow, deep breath, her gaze never breaking from Haley's, her eyes so full of emotion they felt like they might spill over. She took a small step closer, reaching up to gently cup Haley's face, her thumb brushing softly over Haley's cheek as if to make sure she was really there.

"Haley..." Kate whispered, her voice filled with all the unsaid words, all the longing that had built up over the time they'd been apart.

"Yeah?" Haley's voice was barely a whisper, her own breath catching as she looked up at Kate, feeling that familiar, dizzying warmth spreading through her.

"This," Kate murmured, her words soft and deliberate, "this is the part where you stop talking..." Her lips curved into the hint of a smile. "And kiss me again."

Haley's grin widened, her eyes twinkling. "I love this part," she said, her voice light, teasing, but her heart so full it felt like it could burst.

And then, they kissed, a kiss that felt like coming home, like every wish they hadn't even known they'd made had just come true. The world around them faded, the cool air and starry sky blanketing them in perfect, magical silence, as if the night itself held its breath, watching them.

As they stood there wrapped in each other's arms, Haley felt a warmth that went far beyond the holiday cheer. She'd always loved Christmas at the ranch as a kid—the lights, the laughter, the familiar smell of pine and cinnamon. But this moment, here in Kate's arms, was something she could never have dreamed a Christmas could be. It wasn't just a homecoming; it was her heart finding a place to rest, and it was more magical than she ever imagined. For the first time, Christmas wasn't just a memory—it was the beginning of something beautiful and real.

THE END

Made in the USA
Monee, IL
18 October 2025